A Twist of Night and Day

The Asteria Chronicles, Volume 1

Aubrey Winters

Published by Aubrey Winters, 2021.

This book is a work of fiction. The names, characters, and events in this book are the products of the author's imagination. Any similarity to real persons living or dead is coincidental and unintentional. No part of this book may be reproduced in any form or by any electronic or mechanical means, including information storage and retrieval systems, without written permission from the author, except for the use of brief quotations in a book review.

A TWIST OF NIGHT AND DAY

First edition. April 28, 2021.

Copyright © 2021 Aubrey Winters.

Written by Aubrey Winters.

PRONUNCIATION GUIDE

HOW TO SAY...
- Alfynia – Al-fee-nee-ya
- Asteria – Ah-stair-ee-ya
- Astrid – As-trid
- Castiel – Cas-tee-elle
- Elysia – Elle-eye-see-ah
- Euphelia – Yoo-fee-lee-ah
- Forescua – For-es-kiu-ah
- Maven – May-ven
- Ryken – Rai-ken
- Sirona – Sir-oh-na
- Vorukael – Vo-ru-kale

CHAPTER ONE

THERE ARE MANY LESSER fae who aren't as fortunate as I am, so I shouldn't be complaining. I know I'll sound like an ungrateful princess.

But it's not an easy thing to stay positive when I was bullied throughout the Academy for being a halfling. And then my well-meaning mother invites those bullies to a graduation celebration I never wanted.

All faeries, even lesser fae, are immortal—barring fatal injury and illness, of course—but our magic doesn't fully develop until we're about 500 years old. After that, most high fae are sent to the Fae Academy for fifty years of schooling to hone our magical powers and combat skills.

I received fifty years of education alongside fifty years of bullying.

Unless I achieved my lifelong dream of being a Court Enforcer and accepted a contract to take them out, I was ready to leave and never see the inconsiderate, spoiled brats from the Day and Autumn Courts again.

I almost sigh at the thought of finally exacting revenge after all the years of torture—then promptly shake the thoughts away. I'm the heiress to the Night Court. Being an Enforcer is a dream I can never turn into a reality, even if I want it almost as much as I want to never lay eyes on my school bullies again.

But my mother, Queen Maven of the Night Court, bless her heart, wants me to have a graduation worthy of a princess—especially after seeing the parties the other court monarchs threw for their children. It's not her fault she doesn't know about the bullying.

To keep her from worrying too much about her halfling child, I simply never told her. I used to think it was a brilliant plan. Now, with everyone downstairs waiting for me? I can't say it was the right choice.

So here I am, standing in front of my full-length mirror while Nettie laces up the back of my ridiculously poofy dress.

"Are you sure you can't just shape-shift into me and simply *be* me for the evening?" I ask between breaths—because that's how tight this thing is. It's no problem for her bark-like fingers, though. Despite the appearance of small twigs, Nettie possesses more strength than one would expect from her branch-like limbs.

I should know. I've tested her patience enough times while growing up.

"You know I could have my magic stripped. Do you really hate me so much?" She smiles at me in the mirror's reflection. Although her arms and legs bear resemblance to a tree, her face is mostly clear of bark aside from the occasional twig that sticks out of her hair.

I smile back; I'm just teasing her.

We both know she can't pretend to be me. Even if it weren't against the law to shift into another person's image, Nettie is a

A TWIST OF NIGHT AND DAY

lesser faerie. Changing out of her thin, tree-like body is an impossible task for the small amount of magic she possesses.

Her sharp black eyes sparkle, and her thin brown lips pull into a grim smile. The twigs on her head droop a little. She knows about my torturous years at the Academy, but she knows better than to bring it up.

I never want to talk about it.

Her twig-like fingers carefully thread silver leaves into the silver-white hair that she's pulled into elaborate twists and braids atop my head. The leaves blend in with my natural color, giving me a wild yet elegant look.

She passes me several silver and black loops and chains to put into my earlobes and presses pointy silver caps into my palm. As a halfling, my ears are not as sharp as those of full faeries.

It's always been a sore point for me.

These caps top the tips of my ears to give them the appearance of being higher and sharper, and I rarely go anywhere without ear caps.

Plus, they're handy for when I want to spell them with magic and use them as unsuspecting weapons.

Silver and black are the colors of the Night Court. As the only heir to my mother's throne, I am dressed in a long midnight-blue and silver dress and draped in silver and black jewellery. The blue is so dark it shimmers black, like the night sky dotted with stars.

Satisfied, Nettie crouches behind me and takes both my shoulders into her branch-like hands. She looks me in the eye through the mirror and purses her lips. I give a stiff nod.

Steeling myself, Nettie leads me down the grand staircase and into the ballroom. Someone announces my arrival. Everyone quiets. All eyes are on me as I take my time walking to the mezzanine. Not because I savor the attention—far from it. I am worried I will trip and fall in front of everyone who made me look like a fool for half a century.

At my celebration are high fae from all the courts as well as all the fae students of the Academy—including those who graduated with me this year. My tormentors.

At once, the hall explodes with applause.

Warmth flushes my cheeks and for a moment, I feel happy for everyone's attendance.

Until my eyes land on him.

He smirks from the middle of the room. He raises his glass in a fluid motion and dips his golden-haired head in a mock bow.

With him are Princesses Marina and Maryll of the Spring Court and the twins Prince Damian and Princess Darla of the Autumn Court. The royals of Winter and Summer are, to my surprise, not with them.

He is Prince Castiel Ares of the Day Court. My nightmare.

A painfully handsome, bright, and golden exterior hides the devil within. The youngest and wildest of the eight Day Court Ares royalty, he has virtually no chance of becoming the Day King so politically, no one cares about him. His court cowers at his temper, and his family ignores him. If I didn't hate him so much, I might pity him.

But he lashes out, and he likes to take it out on me because of my blood and my status. He thinks a halfling like me isn't worthy of my position as princess. Unfortunately, being half high fae is worse than being full lesser fae in the eyes of many. I'm sure life would have been much different if my mother weren't the Night Queen—I'd still have been treated as inferior, but perhaps a little less violently so. They wouldn't think I was—am—undeserving of my position as the Night Court's heiress.

I never told my mother this. I should be strong enough to handle my own troubles. If I had run to my mother for everything, I would have proved everyone right—and I don't want to be the useless halfling they all see me as.

Only Nettie sometimes caught me crying alone, though she knew I wouldn't say anything so she never asked.

Besides, Castiel's forms of torture were trivial in the grand scheme of things; what's fifty friendless years when you are immortal?

It also helped that every season break, I returned home to my best friends, Elysia and Alfynia.

Elysia is my cousin, another high fae. Alfynia is a foundling—a human child who stumbled into Asteria and tasted our food, guaranteeing that she could never live in the human world again.

Elysia was the one who found Alfynia as an infant. As a child herself, Elysia wanted her new sister to have a similar name to hers.

To this day, no one understands how she came up with Alfynia's name—and one sharp glare from my fierce cousin ensures no one dares to ask.

Sustained on fae food, Alfynia will live forever so long as no fatal harm or illness comes her way and she doesn't spend too much time outside of Asteria. She's been part of my family since.

And although Alfynia has no magic of her own, Elysia and I never found it to be a problem. We love her as our sister and try to give her as many magic imbued items as possible so she may feel safe traveling around Asteria.

While Alfynia became a scholar in her own way, Elysia became a Knight. Unfortunately, neither of them were at the Academy with me. As a human, Alfynia wasn't able to register as a student. Elysia is older, and had already graduated by the time I enrolled. Thus, I would come home every season's break and find solace with my best friends and then steel myself for four more months of solitude.

I suppose this celebration is not only for my graduation, but also for never having to return to the Academy and face the brats from the other courts.

I could drink to that.

The applause dies as I rise from my curtsy, rushing past the copious amounts of lavishly decorated tables, chairs, and elegantly dressed fae to head straight for the banquet table. I don't want to see Castiel's icy blue eyes anymore. I just want what little food I can fit into my stomach with this dress on, and then I want to see my friends. My sisters.

Unfortunately, luck is not on my side today.

Just as the table is within my reach, I suppress a groan. Castiel is at the table's end and Darla stands close to him.

They look like the perfect pair.

Auburn hair piles high on her head, woven with golden strands. Her dress shimmers with the warm colors of fall. Her pointed face looks elegant rather than pinched, and her brown eyes are the color of the sweetest chocolate despite the poison that comes out of her perfectly plump, painted, orange mouth. There's something to be said about fae beauty hiding the ugly within.

She presses herself against Castiel's arm and whispers something in his ear. He only nods curtly in response.

Castiel looks as though he's made of the sun itself. He is dressed in a white and gold suit custom made to fit him perfectly. Intricate gold, yellow, orange, and red designs weave themselves into the cloth by magic so that even from afar, I can see them flickering. Little suns adorn his earlobes, and the pointed tips of his ears are capped with warm colored precious metals. His golden hair needs no adornment but a thin circlet sits atop it anyway, keeping the untamed mass down. His cheekbones are as sharp as they are high.

My heart freezes when he turns his blue eyes to me; they darken with recognition. They're lined by kohl, which emphasizes their smoky indigo hue. They are the color of the sky right before a storm approaches. But I know *he* is the storm.

His lips pull into a sneer. He brushes by Darla and walks toward me.

I want to turn and go, but there are too many people around, and he's already caught sight of me. Straightening my back, I decide to walk into the fire.

I approach the table and pick up a ceramic plate rimmed with silver, pretending the fruit and sweets have my full interest. Pretending I'm not all too aware of his presence and his nearness.

"Congratulations," a silky voice purrs too closely for my liking.

I take my time looking at the fruits; they're drizzled with honey, jams, and other sugars that I can't discern at this moment. All I can truly focus on is how close he is. He smells of cedar by the sea, like an early morning in a forest on a deserted island before the animals are awake.

"Thank you," I say curtly.

"Have you received all of your graduation gifts yet?" He takes a step closer.

I take a step back, pretending to decide between the colorful cakes. They are of various sizes and colors, but each one is topped with a dollop of midnight-blue frosting with sprinkles of silver stars.

"I'm not sure." I just want him to leave. I want to get my food and meet Elysia and Alfynia outside by the pond. It is ridiculous of me to be so afraid of this princeling. He is not the Day King. He is nowhere close to becoming king. Not to mention his influence over both his and other Courts is minimal at best, his command of magic is weaker than most, and his swordsmanship is downright embarrassing.

But there's something about his charm that always makes me feel small, no matter how much more accomplished I am. I've worked my whole life to best every faerie of my generation and yet, it never seems enough.

I am never enough.

"Well, I know for a fact that you haven't received *all* of your gifts yet, flower."

I hate that name. I hate when he calls me that. My name is Astrid, which *is* a flower, but when he says it like that, it reminds me of something weak; something precious and delicate. Something to be protected.

I want more than anything to be the exact opposite.

Even so, the way he says *flower* is unlike the way anyone else says my name, and I shiver unwittingly.

I hate him.

"And how is it you know that?" I counter coolly, proud that none of my inner turmoil makes it to my voice.

He steps forward, and this time I don't step back. He leans down—he's almost a head taller than I—and whispers in my ear.

"My gift to you is waiting at the pond." His hot breath tickles my hair, and his lips are close to brushing the sides of my ear where the caps don't reach.

My heart stops.

It takes all my willpower not to drop the plate and let it shatter. Instead, I place it carefully on the table so as not to cause a scene.

Castiel grins widely and takes a step back as I pick up my ridiculous pile of skirts to walk as quickly—and quietly—as I can. I head toward the main doors which lead to the garden.

My heart pounds as images flood my mind; it is one thing for them to torture me, but another for them to hurt my friends. My family. Elysia can handle herself, but Alfynia! I hope she has her oak bark bracelet. At the least, she should have her rowan berry and elderwood necklace. Still, I worry.

Despite being granted immortality by Asteria's wild natural magic, humans are still susceptible to faerie glamor and charms. Oak bark can provide a brief resistance against faerie magic while rowan berries help humans see past faerie glamor. Elderwood prevents a human from falling under a faerie's charm, which would leave them vulnerable to whatever the faerie wants them to do. Being able to create a protection piece using a combination of items is a rare skill that few possess—it is rarer still to own such a precious item. It was difficult for Elysia and I to get our hands on the necklace Alfynia now wears at all times.

Castiel snickers, his long legs keeping pace with ease. "Are you excited, flower? I spent a long time wondering what to give you."

I snarl and speed up. As soon as I am through the doors, I break into a sprint. My heeled feet tap hard against the stone path.

The gardens are a blur of greens and blues, and I barely acknowledge him as I weave toward the pond.

I spot the tall floral arch of my destination, but the hedges along the side keep the view from me. A soft whimper whispers past the greenery. I reach the arch and gasp.

A fire roars to life in my heart as I struggle to understand the scene before me.

Damian stands with his hazel suit wrapped in intricate gold designs. Marina is at his side, her long, pin straight hair looking blacker against the contrast of her light blue gown. Darla, whom I hadn't noticed leaving the banquet table, stands with them. They circle the pond, laughing gleefully.

Then, I notice the dark brown hair bobbing in the middle of the pond.

At first, I think they've beheaded her and tossed her head in the pond for me to see.

But once I can force my eyes back to the scene, I realize it is horrible—but not as grisly as I'd first imagined.

A TWIST OF NIGHT AND DAY 13

Alfynia treads water in the pond, and her eyes focus solely on Damian. He's charmed her into the water and glamored her so she thinks it's fun.

Who took her protection pieces? How did they get close enough?

I'm about to take off my shoe to wipe the smug look off his face, but Castiel distracts me.

He dangles a bracelet and a necklace before my eyes. "Did you need these?" He snickers.

I bare my teeth and swipe for them, but he is quicker. My heart sinks as I watch Alfynia's oak bracelet plop in the water like stones he has failed to skip.

"Oops," he says. His eyes are a lighter blue against the strong afternoon sun, and they sparkle with mirth. The happier he looks, the angrier I feel.

I will deal with him later.

Kicking off my shoes, I yank the beautiful silk skirt from my waist, not caring about my exposed legs or the expensive fabric. I feel Castiel's hateful, heated gaze, so I throw the skirts at his face.

Without another thought, I dive in.

The chill of the murky waters does nothing to cool the inner fire raging inside of me.

Our pond is huge—it's more like a little lake. Mother likes to collect creatures, and she likes to let them roam our lands and our waters. This particular pond is filled with merdogs: aquatic canines whose bite is laced with a sleeping drug. Our royal healers—who are also our poison masters—personally harvest the saliva from these merdogs every year. Nothing but the best and the freshest for my mother.

But these brats don't know that.

They don't know that the merdog herd will wake from their sleep soon; they likely aren't even aware we have the aquatic canines here. They think it's funny to charm a human to jump into a pond for their pleasure. To glamor my sister for their own entertainment.

I grit my teeth and reach for Alfynia's arm. It's hard to get a good grip on her slippery skin as she treads water.

I take a deep breath and dive back down, reaching for her waist instead.

This time, I succeed and pull her close. She fights back and gives me a dirty glare—I'll admit it stings even though I know she's under Damian's glamor. She pushes me with both hands. I groan and take a deep breath.

Throwing my head underwater, I watch for Alfynia's kicking legs which are exposed beneath her floating skirts. In my periphery, I notice a merdog sleeping with its tail tucked under its snout. A bubble rises from its nose, completely unaware of the chaos happening in its realm.

I gasp for air as I break out of the water and wrap my hands around her wrists. I pull. Damian's laugh is distinctly deeper than Castiel's, but I would know Castiel's dark voice anywhere. They're all laughing at us.

Only Alfynia is important right now.

She's heavier than I anticipated while underwater—especially since she's putting up a fight—so it's a battle for me to keep our heads above water. In between gasps of air, I notice the way Castiel and his friends watch us struggle.

They're too gleeful.

Magic tingles in my fingers. I take one hand off Alfynia's to put up a shield in between gasps of air; a dome of midnight blue spreads above us to deflect any malicious intentions they might try to throw our way.

I finally pull a protesting Alfynia onto land, and I realize why she was so heavy. Damian charmed her into the water with her full dress on. Completely drenched, the gown must weigh an obscene amount. I bite my tongue to hold my anger in check—she could have *drowned!*

She ignores me and looks only to Damian for her next instruction; his lips move as he prepares another charm.

Not again.

I build magic in my fingers as I thread them through the grass behind me.

Without warning, I whip a fistful of the innocuous grass at Damian. My midnight magic appears as flames that wrap around the cluster, transforming them midair from delicate pieces into sharp green miniature daggers. He ducks in time, but is surprised enough that he retracts his magic from Alfynia to focus on disintegrating my magic.

Every faerie has a well of magic they can tap into, but that well is not unlimited. If a faerie were to overstretch their magical limits, they would be incapacitated for a time and forced to rest while the magic recovers.

While Damian's magic is strong, he doesn't have very much of it. I've never seen him hold three spells at once, and glamoring humans takes a lot of power. He couldn't have defended and kept his hold over Alfynia.

Once Damian releases my sister, she slumps to the ground. Unconscious.

Pieces of grass float harmlessly as I pat Alfynia's face. Bits of her hair stick to her pale face and her eyes are closed, but she's breathing. She'll recover from the ordeal.

No one else from the party has noticed that my sister was almost drowned and eaten; merdogs are voracious carnivores who will eat anything in their paths. Not that any of the faeries here would care.

If anyone did notice us out here, I'm not surprised they didn't offer help. Faeries are a selfish bunch who provide help only if it benefits them, as well.

"You had to go and ruin our fun," a voice drawls. "We wanted to see how long a human could tread water before their mortality overcomes them. Such fragile, pathetic things, aren't they?"

Castiel stands with hands in his pockets, ignoring his friends. His eyes have transformed into a dark blue, but they're focused only on me.

He would have let her drown without remorse. I know it.

Years ago, a foundling servant I was fond of, Sam, used to walk me to the Academy every season. Sandy-haired and bright eyed, he was my first kiss. My first love. My first everything.

I didn't care he was mortal, and he didn't care I wasn't. He was a few years older than I, and perfect in every way.

He would walk me to the Academy at the beginning of every season and pick me up at the end. I looked forward to those moments with him almost as much as I looked forward to my sisters.

Until one day, I went to meet him and caught Castiel holding Sam's rowan and elderwood bracelet. He and his friends tortured Sam, making him stuff soap into his mouth and then

A TWIST OF NIGHT AND DAY

forcing him to throw himself off the tallest set of stone stairs at the Academy over and over. Even when poor Sam limped and could barely stand, they charmed him to get back on his feet and walk up the stairs only to fall off of them again.

By the time I found them, Sam had broken both legs and several ribs. He refused to talk to me again after that. I didn't blame him, but my heart and his gait were never quite the same.

And I never forgave Castiel.

He would have let Sam die if I hadn't intervened, just as he would have let his friends kill Alfynia.

As soon as Alfynia blinks awake, I stalk over to Castiel. An ugly sneer mars his otherwise hatefully perfect face. Her necklace is still in his palm. His blue eyes darken further as I approach.

I reach to swipe the necklace from him before he speaks, but he's faster. He isn't a warrior, but he's always been quick.

His long fingers drop the protection piece back into his pockets, and I turn to leave before I make a bigger scene than I already have. This isn't a fight I will win today. His gaze burns holes into my back as I help Alfynia up.

None of them say anything as we exit, but I make sure Castiel sees my glare before we leave.

"Happy graduation," I mutter, picking my way past the ruined remnants of my dress as we head for the side doors to avoid the ballroom's sizable crowds.

THE REST OF THE EVENING is a blur. Elysia keeps Alfynia company as I am forced to mingle after Nettie puts me in another dress, clicking her tongue after seeing what I did with my first one. My new dress is dark red and lined with silver. It's not nearly as exquisite as the first, nor elegant enough for such a grand party.

I don't mind.

I wear it with practiced ease despite the storm of emotions inside of me as I greet and nod and smile when I am supposed to. I leave as soon as I'm not needed.

I tiptoe into Alfynia's room to find my cousin sitting on a chair, reading. Her long white hair has been tied back into a tight braid that lays over her right shoulder. Elysia's not even in her evening wear; she is instead in loose green pants and a tight black sleeveless top. Alfynia is nowhere to be found.

"Where is she?"

"Taking a bath," Elysia studies me with raised eyebrows. "How was the party?"

I ignore her question, knowing she's teasing me. "Are you sure she can take a bath right now? After what happened?" I whisper despite knowing Alfynia can't hear me through the door. Her bedroom has its own ensuite bathroom, and I could hear the running water behind closed doors.

"She was a little pale, but she'll be fine. She's a strong girl." Elysia shakes her head as I pace the room. Fury burns within me, a fire stoked by the memory of what could have happened to our precious sister.

Elysia is right; Alfynia is strong. But she is also mortal without magic of her own, making her susceptible to faerie magic. I only wish my mother would let us hunt for more magical artifacts so we could help Alfynia arm herself with more than a berry bracelet and wooden necklace.

But now that I've graduated, maybe she would finally let me search the lands of Asteria for something—anything—that Alfynia could use for permanent protection.

I stop pacing when the bathroom door opens. The silhouette of our sister emerges from behind the steam.

"Alfynia," I cross the room to hug her. I'm glad to see that her cheeks have color again, even if it's only from the heat of her bath.

"Hey," she greets me, pulling away from my embrace to adjust the towel holding her mass of brown hair.

"I'm so sorry this happened," I sit her down on the bed. Elysia and I stand before her.

"We're hiding berries in your socks and elderwood in the heels of your shoes from now on." Elysia's arms are crossed, but her anger isn't directed at either of us. She's likely mad at herself for not having been there to protect Alfynia; Elysia isn't the type of girl to talk about emotions. She'd much rather tell you how she feels with her fists.

"Better yet, we should see if there's a way we can permanently implant some. Maybe a tattoo with ink of ground berries and elderwood." I rack my brains for artists who work with permanent ink. "I don't know if anyone's tried it before, but I'm sure we can get something to work."

"I love you both." Alfynia wraps her arms around herself and I swallow a whimper from how small she looks. She's beautiful and strong and should never have to feel so small. My magic stirs under my skin, hot with anger, when I think of what I want to do to Castiel and his friends for making my sister feel this way. "Will you do something for me?"

We nod vigorously. Even if her eyes weren't so big and sad, we could never say no to our human sister. Though the three of us are from different mothers, anyone would be hard-pressed to find blood-sisters closer than we three.

"Just sit with me for a while." Alfynia pats at the space next to her on the bed, and we climb in under the sheets with her immediately.

We spend the rest of the night gossiping and laughing about which faerie lord or lady is sleeping with which, helping Alfynia forget the incident. We help her forget that she's not quite the same as the rest of us.

But as my sisters fall asleep, an idea hatches in my mind. I can't shake it, nor can I tell them what it is. Neither would approve of me carrying out the plan alone, but both would be even more unlikely to help me. So I wait until they're sound asleep before I sneak out of bed in the middle of the night.

CHAPTER TWO

THE NIGHT IS DARK AND chilly, but you don't grow up as princess of the night without growing to love the inky sky. Many, even those in the Night Court, love the sun and the light as well, but I find comfort in the shadows.

Confidence washes over me when I glance at the moon; I think the reason I love the night sky is mostly because of the moon. As a child, I was often alone. I spent many nights awake and staring at the bright silvery sphere. Her light would wash over me, and I knew I would be okay. It's always been a beacon of shining hope.

The moon tonight is a sliver that barely peeks through the clouds, but I'm grateful. The less light there is, the easier I will blend in with the night. I'm dressed in all black: lightweight leggings with a loose top tucked into leather straps that wrap around my waist. I have an assortment of daggers tucked into leather sheaths that sit on the straps running across my body.

More leather covers my wrists, ensuring support for hand-to-hand combat. I've tied my silver hair with a cord and pinned the loose pieces, tucking it all under a dark hood. While I normally love my hair, I know it's a detriment to the career I desire. It's hard to blend into the night when your head is a glowing beacon showing where you are.

I glide silently through the castle grounds, knowing that I risk the peace treaty between all our courts—except the Dark Court—if I am caught.

But I won't be. And even if I were, Castiel would never be such a coward as to tell anyone that I broke in. He has more pride than that.

My mother has spelled the Night Castle against realmwalking, so I have to leave the castle grounds before I can let the metallic tang of magic fill the air. As soon as I step past the wards, shadows raise from the ground like mist, climbing the air as though it were a living being before completely enveloping me.

For a long second, I am engulfed in pure darkness. Echoes from past faeries lost to the Other Realm fill my ears, asking me to join them. For a heartbeat, I am tempted—as every faerie is—but instead of succumbing to the voices, I take a step away and my foot lands on solid ground.

I take another and walk out of the shadows, leaving them behind.

Realmwalking is a dangerous mode of transportation, albeit handy in a pinch. Every time a faerie walks through the natural world and into the shadows of the Other Realm, we're tempted by the faeries who succumbed to the Void. The Void that lives in the Other Realm feeds on the souls of lost faeries; if we're not careful, we fall prey to it and become one of those voices, never able to leave the Other Realm again.

I emerge at the gates of our court, having realmwalked past the main city that lies between the Night Castle and our borders. The stone walls that border our court are high—taller than any faerie can jump. And even then, another barrier extends invisibly toward the sky, rippling with the magic that circles and protects our lands.

Letting my hood fall back a shade, the guard recognizes me immediately and steps aside. We nod curtly at each other, and I cross into the Courtless.

The Courtless is a neutral land ungoverned by any court laws. It is also without restrictions on realmwalking. Once again, I call forth the inky darkness and step into the shadows. Again, I hesitate before stepping out and away from the Void's calls. The Other Realm fades as I emerge from it to enter a forest.

I'm at the edge of the woods with an unobstructed view of the Day Court's borders. Stones which make up the walls are free of moss; there is usually too much sun here for it to grow. Unlike our borders, the Day's walls extend only about the height of three faeries. Anyone adept enough with magic could easily propel themselves over the borders—especially since I can't even see ripples of invisible barriers extending from the tops of these walls.

The moon is high in the sky now, its sliver still powerful enough to bleach the grass of color. Two guards slump against the walls at the gate.

I scoff. Security really means nothing to the Day Court. The tang of magic is in the air, so at least they have wards of some sort.

Testing the weight of a small stone nearby, I throw it far in the opposite direction of where I hide. Neither guards stir, so I try another heftier stone.

Three stones later, I decide they must be too drunk to notice—it seems like something the Day Court's sentries would do, given their lax security measures. Perhaps they wouldn't notice me slipping through, either.

Although I briefly entertain the idea of simply walking right by them, I decide it's safer to glamor myself and hope neither wake up to see through it.

I hold my breath and wait until I feel the tingle of magic on my skin; I don't have a mirror to check how I look now, but I know it should be enough of a disguise. I taste metal and wait until the air shifts and ripples around me to make myself invisible. It's rare that someone would have on their person both rowan berries and elderwood, but I'm taking precautions against both.

A part of me wants to play with fire and see what would happen if I threw caution to the wind. The other more rational part says I need to get Alfynia's protection piece back. I have a mission, and I need to succeed. Otherwise, how could Alfynia feel safe in Asteria? In her own home?

I walk past the drunken guards, taking care to slump my shoulders and look down. Something doesn't feel right, but I bite my tongue and keep my eyes trained on the ground.

Something seems wrong... But I have to remember the mission. Don't risk getting caught.

I keep my head down and shuffle my feet just enough to look inconspicuous, but not enough to draw attention. They don't even stir in their sleep.

Like the Night Castle, the main city surrounds Day's Castle, where the monarchs live.

The cobblestones are damp enough that slivers of light reflect where small pools gather.

It's late. The streets are empty, but I duck into an alley anyway. Almost every window is dark; no one is awake.

I let magic pool in my belly and taste the familiar tang in the air. Shadows rise from the ground like fumes curling in on themselves, climbing until I see nothing but darkness.

I step in.

Whispers call me; temptation swarms the back of my head and fills my mind. The Void and the lost fae beg me to stay and be their salvation. I close my eyes and step away from them. Toward the Day Court's castle.

Castiel's home is almost as grand as mine—grander, in some ways. Whereas my mother ensures we are always ready for battle, Day Court favors grandeur over practicality.

I scoff at the twin decorative towers that flank the front door. So many vulnerabilities. They've made their walls from stone, but their doors are wooden and not reinforced. Their wards against realmwalking end at their doors rather than at the end of their grounds.

Easier for me to infiltrate, I guess.

No one guards the doors, so I enter uninterrupted. Their castle is eerily quiet, but perhaps that's to be expected, given that I've broken into someone's home in the middle of the night. My anxious mind is likely making the silence seem louder than it truly is.

I've been in the main parts of the Day Court's castle before. Every royal faerie has been here; monarchs throw massive parties every year and invite every court to join. I never stayed long because I didn't like being in my tormentor's home. Who would?

But if I'd known then what I know now, I'd have taken better care to survey the castle more thoroughly for reconnaissance—but I didn't think I'd ever be here uninvited.

Enormous paintings of past Day monarchs decorate the halls. Castiel's parents stare into space with their crowns of gold.

The next portraits are of Castiel's siblings: seven portraits of high cheeked, golden eyed faeries looking into space. Mavis, Raven, Uriah, Bronson, Emelia, Angelica, and Corin. Mavis, Emelia, Angelica, and Corin each have similar golden curls, whereas Raven, Uriah, and Bronson have cropped blond hair. Only Castiel, whose portrait seems to have been added as an afterthought, looks less than perfect. He sports messy golden hair like he was dragged out of bed against his will. He's also the only one looking down at me, as though in contempt.

I feel my lip curl inadvertently at his sneer and immediately feel silly; I'm angry at a painting. But even his painting looks at me with condescension. I swallow hard and throw a rude gesture at it before moving on.

I'm looking for his room, but I've never been in these parts of the castle before—I'd only ever been in the main ballroom—but common sense tells me I've entered the entertainment side of their castle. I only need to make my way to the residential wing.

I don't pass a single servant, so I find the throne room quickly and undisturbed: a large, ornate door decorated with gold trim representing the sun and its rays.

My heart flutters.

It is slightly ajar.

A TWIST OF NIGHT AND DAY

My stomach is in knots, and something doesn't feel right, but I squash the feeling. The throne room is usually at the center of castles, which means the residential wing should be on the other side. I'm about to move past it when something catches my attention.

An awful sound—like someone groaning in pain—comes through the doors and I freeze.

Cursing, I steady my breath. It's probably the wind. It's likely nothing—

"*Ugnn.*"

I creep closer, curiosity getting the better of me. Peering through the door, I gasp.

My hands turn clammy, and a lump forms in my throat.

The bodies of royals lay on the ground, broken and bleeding—so different from their elegance painted in the hallways. Some are twisted unnaturally. Others—I can't even recognize them.

I want to throw up, but I dare to bring my gaze further and immediately wish I hadn't.

A dark-haired, fair-skinned young man—a faerie—has his foot on the chest of his victim. Black whorls and patterns mar the side of his face: the exile mark of the Dark fae.

Crimson coats his victim's blond hair. Narrowed blue eyes stare up past the tip of the sword that's pointed at his throat.

My breath catches when I realize who the victim is.

"Little princeling Ares. Such a big family, and all that's left is *you*," the Dark faerie coos maliciously, taunting Castiel and poking the day prince's throat with every word.

"You're sure this is what you want?" Castiel drawls. I want to scoff. Even facing death by the blade, he's arrogant and full of unsubstantiated confidence.

I should leave. I should run straight home and let Mother know the Dark fae have overtaken the Day Court. We need to ready ourselves in case they come for us. At the very least, we need to find out *why* the Dark fae have decided to attack.

Peeling my eyes from the horrendous sight, I've resolved to leave when the Dark faerie speaks as I take my first step.

"Your confidence astounds me. Even facing death, you're annoying."

I agree. Castiel is a pain.

I take another step.

"I hope you love your family. You're about to see them again."

I close my eyes for a second.

Only a split second.

But before a heartbeat has passed, I've already whirled around. The door is wide open.

My blade flies out of my hand, wrapped in midnight magic.

It sails silently through the air even as I watch it, wondering just what I've done.

It makes a horrible sound when it hits its mark. It will be some time before the squelch stops haunting my dreams.

Castiel's cerulean eyes meet mine. His jaw opens slightly, but I'm already on the move before the Dark faerie's body even hits the ground.

I should run the other way.

I should pretend like I saw nothing.

I should leave him to his fate.

A TWIST OF NIGHT AND DAY

But I'm running to him like the fool that I am.

Before I give Castiel my hand, I wrench my dagger out from the Dark faerie's face and wipe the blood on his clothes, looking away from his glassy eyes. I swallow the bile that threatens to rise.

"Hurry *up*," I snarl at the princeling.

He stares at me, speechless and stupid. I curse and yank him to his feet.

"Did I misunderstand? Did you *want* to die?" I hiss.

His mouth opens and closes without a sound, and I sigh. I've made a mistake. I shouldn't have saved him.

"You can come with me or you can stay here. I don't care either way." I huff and turn to leave, ignoring the bodies of his family. I might hurl right here if I look too closely, and I'm acutely aware of how precarious this situation already is. I have no idea how many more Dark faeries roam the halls, and I don't need to attract attention.

Thankfully, the idiot prince follows me.

"Do you have Alfynia's necklace?" I thrust my hand out as soon as we're through the throne room doors so I can see down both ends of the hall in case more Dark faeries arrive. It might sound stupid, but I refuse to return home empty-handed—not when I'm already here. Not when I saved his life and potentially became entangled in this mess. I will at least return with what I originally came for.

Thankfully, he doesn't protest and nods mutely.

I know I just saved his life and killed a faerie with a single dagger. I know I've perfected sculpting my face into one that incites fear and commands respect. I know I have no reason to fear him, *especially* in this moment.

On the inside, though, I feel like a pile of mush barely holding together. I just want to go home.

Castiel doesn't speak at all. He only swallows hard before reaching into his pockets and putting the precious necklace in my hands.

I try not to let out a sigh of relief. We can easily replace the bracelet. The necklace, though? Losing it would be a blow that would take a long time from which to recover.

I put it on and tuck it safely under my shirt, then tell him to guide us out of here. Again, he does so silently.

A small part of me aches for him. To lose your entire family in one night... I might not know what that's like, but I know what I see on his face, hidden behind his emotionless mask.

His brows are drawn, and the usual sneer is missing from his frown. He has yet to say a single word, and that unnerves me.

I'm used to an abrasive and arrogant Castiel Ares. The one who has more confidence than I've ever known in my entire life.

This quiet and uneasy Castiel—who seems more like a lost child than the man who tormented my first and only lover—makes me sympathetic for him in ways I never wanted to be for such a hateful character.

I curse myself for being so weak. I should have just left him there to die and run home to report what I'd seen. Maybe I'm too weak. Maybe I don't have what it takes to be an Enforcer after all.

But if I'm not fit for a queen and I can't be an Enforcer, who could I be?

I brush the thoughts away—I have to focus on getting out of here alive first.

Castiel holds up a hand before we turn a corner, and we stop to listen.

A woman's whimpering almost sends me around the corner and flying down the halls, but the sudden silencing of her cries gives me pause.

I blink away tears.

See? I could never be a queen.

A true queen worthy of the title would have gone to save the girl; a queen wouldn't have hesitated. An assassin—an Enforcer—hides in the shadows, focusing only on her mission.

I look at Castiel's golden head.

And I failed at that, too.

We crouch by the corner until my legs burn. Finally, Castiel motions for us to continue.

I hope to be spared the sight—and guilt—of the female's body.

Castiel's eyes are cast downward the entire time we move, and both of us strain our ears.

It seems like an eternity passes before the twinkling stars finally greet us as we step out of the castle walls and feel the icy breeze against our faces.

Castiel stares at the moon; the sliver of light makes his blue eyes look so pale, they're almost silver. I can see they're glassy with unshed tears.

Still, he says nothing.

He catches me staring and turns away.

"Can you realmwalk?" His voice is so gravelly I don't even realize he's speaking at first.

When he asks again, I nod dumbly.

"Then you should leave. Go home. It's not safe here." He doesn't meet my eyes when he says this. He looks anywhere but at me.

That he is telling me to leave doesn't register in my mind—what my stupid, soft heart does register is how young he looks. Grief doesn't age him; it does the opposite. Watching his family's murder makes him younger, and he looks lost. I realize he looks how he often made me feel.

And I didn't like feeling that way.

No one should feel that way.

I huff. "And where are you going?"

He blinks. "It doesn't matter."

My arms cross almost of their own accord. I can feel frustration bubbling, but it's not at him. I'm frustrated with myself.

This faerie tormented me throughout our years at the Academy. He tortured and drove away my first love. He hurt my sister.

And yet, I couldn't leave him like this.

Would Alfynia be mad that I helped him? Likely not. She's the kindest of us all. Still, I feel guilt.

"If you make it back home before sunrise, no one will know you were here."

His comment startles me, and I check the moon's position again. He's right. It's already low on the horizon, and soon the sun will replace it. How could I have missed that?

"Are you going to Spring or Autumn?" I assume the twins would help him. Or Darla. She seems infatuated enough.

He scoffs and turns his gaze away, stuffing his hands into his pockets, trying to suppress a shiver. He's dressed in only a cotton short-sleeve shirt and loose dark pants tucked into the tops of fur-lined boots. Comfortable clothing for relaxing at home, if you ignore the blood splatters. Though I am dressed in few layers as well, I am warmed by the adrenaline. I suppose faeries of the Day Court rarely experience winters the way we at the Night Court get them.

"Neither."

"Why not?"

He can't have nowhere to go.

He can't do this to me.

"They wouldn't know what to do." He shuffles his feet, and I feel my resolve cracking.

Don't do this to me.

"They can't help you?" *Or is it that they won't?*

"You're running out of time." He crosses his arms and finally meets my eyes. They're dry, but I see the semblance of something in them. Hopelessness, I think. Despondence.

I let out a growl and stomp over, grabbing his arm. He takes a step back, but my hands are firm on his elbow.

Smokey black rises from the ground and he protests, but my grip is solid—unlike my resolve.

The voices of the lost fae fill our ears, and he hesitates.

He hesitates for longer than I'm comfortable with, and for a fleeting moment, I fear he's going to stay behind in the Other Realm. I lace my fingers through his and dig my nails into the back of his hand.

Dark blue eyes swing to meet mine. Understanding passes between us—or something akin to it—and I see him return to me. We take a step together.

Smoky purples and blues that shimmer black replace the darkness.

We're in the forest of the Courtless. Before us are the walls of the Night Court.

Silent questions dance in his eyes, but now it's my turn to look away. "Letting anyone else murder you would be a disservice to the years I suffered in silence. If anyone's going to kill you, it's going to be me."

I walk toward our gates and hope he follows. I don't think I could explain why I brought him to the Night Court. I don't even understand it myself.

I almost pause and turn around, but then hesitant steps follow me.

Nodding to the guards, I enter our gates with Castiel in tow.

CHAPTER THREE

I PACE ALFYNIA'S ROOM while she and Elysia stare at me wide eyed from the edge of Alfynia's bed.

"You did what?" Alfynia asks at the same time Elysia sputters. "Who's in the next room?"

"How many times do we need to go over this?" I tug on the ends of my braids. "I couldn't leave him."

"Think of what he did to Alfynia," Elysia pauses. "No, wait. Just think about what he did to *you*."

I stop pacing and groan, putting my face in my hands. "I know. You don't have to remind me."

"Clearly, we do." Elysia stands. Her hand rests on her forehead, and she can't even look at me.

"You didn't see him," I say between my fingers. "He was literally facing death."

"And you spared him?" Elysia's brown eyes look upwards. "Sirona help me," she mutters under her breath, asking our wild goddess for the patience to deal with me.

I don't blame her.

"I..."

I don't know why I did it.

"I'm soft," I sink onto the ground, leaning my full weight against the wall.

"You are," Alfynia gets up and crouches in front of me. "But you're also kind. It's what makes you so great."

"You're only saying that because I got your precious artifact back," I mumble between my fingers.

Her laugh is lovely and raises my spirits for a moment. "Yes, but I also mean it."

"How am I going to tell mother?"

"You'll have to admit to breaking into the Day Court..." Elysia pauses and looks at the door, eyes narrowing.

Alfynia and I stand as the door creaks open. Magic flourishes from my fingertips and my muscles tense, fearing the Dark fae somehow broke through our plethora of wards and alarms.

"Admitting to breaking the treaty won't be an issue unless I make it one, considering I'm the only one left of my family. For now." Castiel leans against the door frame, looking haggard. Blood still splattered on his shirt and in his hair.

I stand up. "Did something happen?"

He smiles wryly. "Has it not already?"

I let out a shuddering breath, the gory images flashing in my mind. "Right."

Alfynia stands between me and Elysia, silent but also not sending him away.

None of us have forgotten his actions earlier today, but what does a person say to someone whose entire family was murdered brutally before his eyes?

"I know what you're thinking," he says, his eyes looking out into the night sky through the window. "You're thinking, 'why is he here?'" His eyes, a blue so dark they're almost black, leave the window and meet mine. "Why did you bring me here, Astrid?"

"I told you. If anyone's going to—"

"I don't need your pity." Anger flashes in his midnight eyes, and his voice comes out a low growl. "My family was a wretched lot, and the world is better off without them."

Behind the anger, I see flashes of hurt, and maybe even fear. We are all well-versed enough in the history of the Dark fae. They betrayed the old King Eldritch before the courts were formed over two thousand years ago, so he marked them for their betrayal and sent them into exile. All subsequent Dark faeries are born with the mark. Over five hundred years ago, they broke into and brought ruin to the now extinct Lunar Court, absorbing the Lunar lands into their own after committing genocide on all the Lunar fae.

They do not have a monarch and live with constant chaos, wild and free. Unless someone can Challenge and win against the Dark faeries who led the attack, without a proper monarch, the Day Court will descend into ruins and extinction as well.

And we all know Castiel does not have the skills to win in any combat Challenge, nor does he have someone he can use as a champion to win in his name.

I wouldn't know what to do if I were in his shoes.

"We should wake my mother," I say begrudgingly.

Because even as much as I hate him, as much as I cannot forget the crimes he's committed against me and my family, I am soft. I am weak. I cannot let him walk back home to die—not without at least trying to help.

"Just let me go home." He sags against the door frame. His voice is weak, and it bothers me.

It shouldn't, but it does. It doesn't sound right.

"We're going to get mother," I say again firmly. I turn to give Elysia a look, and she understands. She takes Alfynia's hand and leads our sister back to bed. I bid both of them goodnight before leaving the bedroom, confident that Castiel will follow.

MOTHER IS THE MOST beautiful lady I've ever seen. Though she is fair and silver-haired like me, I could never have enough confidence to carry myself the way she does. She commands the attention of every room, whereas I want to slink into the shadows and avoid eye contact.

I'm told that she showed up at the castle of the Night Court five hundred years ago with a baby in her arms—me. No one knew who she was or where she came from, but everyone bowed to her when she invoked the Challenge against the previous Night King and won.

The crown is passed down in two ways: through lineage or through Challenge. Even if a faerie is born into royalty, it can easily be taken away by someone else more capable through a Challenge by combat. The monarch can use a champion to fight in their stead, but the Challenger must fight for themselves.

That's why Castiel needs help. The Dark faeries who took over his court are now in the position of authority, which means he would be the Challenger—and everyone knows his fighting skills are laughable at best.

Mother won against the Night King's champion, then against the Night King himself when he refused to concede.

She is the goddess I can never be.

She looks down at us from her throne of inky black smoke. It rejects everyone but the Night Queen or King. As a child, I once tried to test the theory and landed right on my bottom, falling through the throne as though it were made of actual smoke.

"What is the Ares boy doing here?" Mother is not amused. It is too early to be awake, but too late to return to bed.

"Mother." I take a deep breath. "The Dark fae have attacked and conquered the Day Court. I thought you would want to know at once."

"My darling," my mother waves a perfectly manicured hand in the air. "We do not need to worry about the Dark fae here. We are secure and ready at all times."

I stiffen when she looks at Castiel again. "So, what is it you're doing here?"

"I'd like to know the same myself." He crosses his arms and I feel warmth rush to the tips of my ears. I wish I could just let him walk back to his crumbling castle.

"In one night, he witnessed his family slaughtered. I thought... I thought we could help him." I purse my lips, ready for reproach.

Instead, my mother simply raises her eyebrows. "What are we supposed to do for them?" She pauses and amends her question. "For him?"

Beside me, Castiel clenches his jaw at the reminder that he's all alone now. Pity worms its way into my heart despite my best efforts. I clench my fists tighter, sure that my nails were digging small semi circles into my palms.

"I don't know. I was hoping you could help in that regard..." I chew my lip.

Castiel bristles next to me and opens his mouth to speak, but my mother promptly silences him with a hand. She looks out the window, watching the night lighten as she thinks.

"There is one way..." She mulls to no one in particular. "Yes, I think it could work."

She turns her shrewd eyes back to us and there is the sparkle of inquisition in them when she pins her eyes on Castiel.

He shifts in his spot.

"Have you ever heard of the Trial Challenge?" Her eyebrow raises and there's the hint of an excited grin on her face.

Though her gaze is directed at him, we both shake our heads. Fae history is long, but we aren't taught much of it in school because faeries are immortal. Why learn about history when those who lived it are still alive to tell the tales?

That's what the Academy instructors tell us, anyway. I don't agree with this sentiment; mistakes are too easily repeated when we rely solely on the memories of faeries who are so old that they've grown apathetic to life and the world around them.

As such, there are many old fae laws that have been forgotten. Castiel and I are part of the newer generation of fae taught only about one type of Challenge: Challenge by combat.

When the old King Eldritch used Asteria's natural magic to bind monarchs to their courts thousands of years ago, he didn't forget to ensure balance through the Challenges so monarchs could be dethroned at any time.

Castiel can Challenge the leaders of the Dark fae for his throne, he wouldn't win because he can't use a champion to make up for his lack of fighting skills.

Neither of us realized there are other ways to dethrone or reclaim a monarch's position.

"It is part of the Old Laws from when the courts were first formed. Unfortunately, there is no way of knowing if the magic of this law is still active until you try to invoke it. If you're lucky, you'll be able to call upon the Trial Challenge."

Mother is an old creature—far older than she looks, much like most fae—so I'm not surprised she is privy to knowledge that neither Castiel nor I were taught.

Because of our immortality, things take a long time to change. Traditions carry on for thousands of years before the possibility of another is accepted or even considered. As such, the Old Laws—if anyone even remembered them—were not deactivated immediately. Even if the older fae were open to change, all the court monarchs need to agree in order to siphon the magic from a law. They rarely agree on anything.

Castiel is still looking away, studying the tiles, but my mother continues undeterred.

"Unlike Challenges by combat which require fighting, the Trial Challenge allows the Challenger to undertake an impossible task or quest dreamed up by the Challenged. If the Challenger can complete the task," my mother says, waving her fingers in the air. "Then they may receive one wish—even if what they desire is the crown. It is a sort of last-effort for those who are about to lose their throne."

The silence that blankets the room is deafening.

"What if..." Castiel pauses, mulling over his words before bringing his gaze up to meet my mother's. "What if I don't want to be King? What if I let someone else Challenge the throne?"

Her lips part slightly, and her eyebrows raise. "You don't have a choice."

"Why not?"

"There is no one else who can do this in your stead. Will you let your family die in vain?"

"Then let them have the court." He averts his gaze. "Let the Dark fae do as they wish."

A fire ignites in my mother's eyes. "You've seen the ruins of the Lunar Court, princeling. You know what the Dark fae can do once they have a court in their clutches."

I see the pain in his eyes before he closes them. His hands are clenched into fists at his side.

The Lunar Court was once lauded and well-respected—until a horde of Dark fae led by a mysterious pair descended upon them one night after a court-wide celebration. Once the Dark faeries murdered all of the high Lunar faeries, they captured the remaining lesser faeries as servants, leaving the court to wither and rot without a proper monarch. To this day, no one knows why the Lunar faeries were unable to fight back. Without a proper monarch, the Day Court is likely to descend into a slow, but inevitable, destruction.

"Why should I care?" He whispers. "A family that didn't care about me. A court that paid me no mind."

Despite myself, I flinch. These are the words of a hurt man. Someone who's taken years of pain and squirreled it away just to survive another day. I know this pain.

A TWIST OF NIGHT AND DAY

He caused me this pain.

And still, I pity him.

Even my mother's face softens as she listens. "My dear, you must. For these are your people, whether you want them. Whether they want you. Until you renounce your throne, the magic of your court calls you. If it hasn't yet, it will soon. And without a proper monarch, the court will lose its ties to Asteria's natural magic. It will crumble and fail with or without the Dark fae."

His jaw twitches, and my mother's eyes narrow. "You have seen the devastation of the Lunar Court."

He hesitates before he speaks. "I will do what I can, and no more."

WE ARE SILENT AS I accompany him to the edge of our grounds and stroll toward the gates. Our city is bustling and alive—awake since before the crack of dawn. By now, the sun shines fiercely overhead, its light unaware of last night's devastation.

He turns his gaze to me as we stand outside my gates. The guards have respectfully turned away to give us privacy, though we're far enough into the Courtless that they wouldn't hear us, anyway. Quietly, I marvel to myself at all the different shades I've noticed in his eyes. Today, they're icy blue with a hint of fear that isn't betrayed by his voice.

"Come with me," he says.

His words are sharp and cold, and they remind me of our days at the Academy even though his eyes didn't look like this back then. Then, they were filled with disdain and a passionate hatred that I never quite understood. Now, I can't figure out anything past the shadows of uncertainty tainted by fear.

His jaw clenches when I don't reply, but he doesn't budge.

His eyes turn pleading in a way I know he could never voice, and I can feel my resolve crumble.

Again.

I'm so weak.

"Why?" I croak.

"You're the best warrior of our generation. Whatever they ask of me—if this even works—I will have to do. Your mother was right." He turns his gaze to the branches swaying in the wind. His hair ruffles in sync. "I can feel the call of my court. It's weak. But I... I have no choice. And it won't be long before the Dark fae come for me, anyway."

There is a special bond between a ruler and their court. Because the courts are fae-made and not natural to Asteria, they don't inherently have magical ties to the land. The monarch becomes the court's connection to Asteria's natural magic, so every structure—even the health of the court itself—depends on the monarch.

I've never experienced the pull of the court because my mother is still strong and healthy; if she were to die—Sirona forbid—and no one took the throne, the Night Court would not survive for long. If the court feels that the current monarch is weakening, it will automatically reach out to the next heir to strengthen its bond to Asteria's wild magic.

Now that Castiel is the only remaining heir for his court, the land will call for him until he resigns his throne or accepts it and protects it until its next ruler.

I feel my face twist with an ugly emotion. How dare he?

A TWIST OF NIGHT AND DAY 45

I am doubtful that one call from his court and he is a changed faerie. He's spent so much of our lives hurting me, and now he wants my help?

How dare he?

"Why should I help you?" My question comes out as a snarl without meaning to.

He blinks in shock and almost takes a step back. Even I am surprised at the animosity in my voice, but my heart is angry and hurt. How dare he torment me and use me on his whim?

"Please," he finally begs, his voice thick with emotion as though he has to choke out the word. "If we—*when* we—succeed, what do you want in return?"

"You think you can buy me off after having tortured me all these years?" A fire ignites in my chest.

"You saved me despite those years," he responds. There is a fire in his eyes too, but his burns with desperation and hatred. Hatred not for me, but for himself. For having to ask me for help because he has no one else to which he could turn.

I am his last and *only* choice, and we both know it.

I let out a shuddering breath.

"What do you want?" He asks again.

He takes my silence as encouragement to continue. He expertly wipes the emotion from his face and, once again, becomes the sly faerie with whom I am all too familiar. The one who charms with words, hurts others, and strikes bargains that benefit only himself.

"I know you want something, Astrid." His eyes narrow slightly, and I can barely feel the delicate magic he's threading into his words. It's not of the same combative nature I'm used to, and it's not a strong magic by any means, but it is a skilled one to be sure. It requires precision and attention to detail that few can manage. While Castiel is not skilled in combat, he has always been a charmer—which often is much deadlier than strength and power alone.

"Don't do that," I snap.

His eyes widen for a moment before a lazy grin spreads over his face. I imagine few catch his persuasion in action.

"But there is, isn't there?" His voice is normal again: deep, rich, and full of promises. I can understand why people are instinctively drawn to him. Coupled with his persuasive magic, I would even hazard to say he doesn't *need* to be good with swords. Why put yourself in the line of danger when you can charm others to fight for you?

My chest tightens uncomfortably and I look away, knowing the implication of what I'm about to say. I swallow hard.

Once. Twice.

Licking my lips, I finally speak. "I don't want to be Queen."

His blond brows shoot up into his unstyled bangs.

"Go on..."

"If we can win this—"

"*When* we win this," he interrupts.

"—then you have to make me your Enforcer." Though we are far into the Courtless fields, my eyes still flicker, worried someone might have heard me.

He drags his eyes up and down my body. His brows furrow in contemplation.

When he finally speaks, his words are slow and careful, as if checking to see whether he had heard me correctly. "So, you would rather come to my court and work for me as my second-in-command... than be Queen of the night?"

He probably thinks I'm out of my mind and is already regretting his offer. While it's a great privilege to be the monarch's Enforcer—because there are certain things that need to be done in the shadows—it's nothing compared to being the actual monarch.

"No one else is brave enough to take Queen Maven's only daughter and block her royal line." It's common knowledge that many have Challenged my mother, and none have succeeded. Everyone expects I will inherit the throne.

His eyebrows arch again. "No one else would be so stupid."

"So, are you stupid or are you brave? You only need to be one of the two to make this work."

A dark grin flashes. One that is weary and wicked and determined all at once. He lets out a long breath. "Stupidity and bravery are but two sides of the same coin."

"So, do we have a deal?" I grin, but my heart pounds at the thought of his acceptance. We don't even know if the Trial Challenge is still active, and I'm already taking steps toward rejecting my queenship. Refusing the title itself is too disrespectful to my mother and all she's accomplished—but perhaps if I left for another well-respected position, it might be acceptable. Besides, joining another court might help open her mind to working with others.

If his Challenge is activated, we would have to see it through to the end. If we succeed, I would resign my claim to the throne. I'm not sure which scares me more.

I swallow hard, thinking of my mother's response. She would never approve, but even she can't fight the magic of a deal.

"Deal," he grins. "I agree to let you join my court with me, in whatever position you desire other than the throne, once I am King of Day Court. Do you agree?"

I wipe my sweaty palms against the soft fabric of my pants and lick my lips, hoping he doesn't realize how nervous I am.

"I agree," I hear myself say.

"We have an accord."

Neither of us move, but we both taste metal in the air as the magic of a bargain twirls around us invisibly, sealing our transaction. Sealing our fate.

Once the tingle of magic subsides, he grins—weary, but determined.

CHAPTER FOUR

THE DAY COURT'S PALACE looks fine from the outside, but I can feel the air crackling with anxiety. It's only been one night, but the court can already feel the void of its missing monarch.

In the daytime, the palace is gorgeous. Bright, tall white walls. Arches that reach for the sky. Towers on each side trimmed with red and gold. Vines climb its exterior with small orange flowers dotting across their lengths. Huge, leafy trees sparkle with golden flecks.

It's as if the palace is built from sunlight itself.

Other than some withering hedges along the ground—the first sign of a court's decline—and the lack of guards, there is no evidence of last night's massacre.

Before we continue, Castiel raises a finger. I stop, looking at him curiously. He opens a hand and spreads his fingers; warm sparkles whirl over his body, covering his casual, loose clothes with gold until I can barely see him anymore.

When they fade, he's dressed in a fitted white shirt with golden threads woven throughout the sleeves from his shoulders to his wrists. Similar intricate decorations adorn the hem of his white pants. Golden leaves weave themselves into his blond locks as golden caps cover the tips of his pointed ears and several rings fit themselves onto his fingers.

The light outfit makes his skin look more tanned than usual.

A confident and cold smile that matches his icy blue eyes settles on his face as though he's in his element. As though he's just returning home from a night of parties.

As though nothing is wrong.

He nods and we continue, silent.

As we approach the embellished front doors, they open of their own accord as if recognizing that the Day Prince has returned home.

He leads me through the halls that look so different in the light, but my attention is not on the décor.

Despite all that has happened, Castiel's back is straight, and he manages a haughty, carefree look as we enter the throne room.

Signs of last night's carnage are still apparent here, though someone has cleared the room of all the bodies.

A slender Dark faerie dressed in a silky black sleeveless gown sits on the cracked throne. Beside her, the bigger throne lies haphazardly on the ground, broken—as though she picked the one she wanted and didn't want anyone to have even her rejects.

A delicate chin rests on her hand, her nails painted as red as her lips. Long black hair cascades past her shoulders in waves as violet eyes stare down at us with contempt.

At first, I think her dress extends to cover her neck, but then I realize her neck is entirely exposed. The skin there and on her upper torso is almost completely covered by tight, intricate black designs. Her exile mark.

She looks young—young enough to be our age. But with faeries, looks can be deceiving.

Castiel leans back on his heels. His head lolls slightly and a lazy smirk grows. The picture of insouciance even as enemies have swarmed his home and murdered his family.

"Ah," the woman scrunches her nose at us. "Have you come to renounce?"

Castiel blinks slowly. "What gives you that impression?"

I almost flinch from the haughtiness in his voice; it reminds me of when he used it with me.

"You've lost your family," she raises an arm. "You've lost your throne." Her other arm raises and sweeps across the wreckage that is the throne room. "What could you possibly have left?" Her voice is sweet, but I know it drips with venom.

Castiel smirks, and the sparkle of persuasion sprinkles his voice. "I invoke the Trial Challenge."

His cold voice, brimming with unfound confidence, echoes in the carnage of the room.

I hardly dare to breathe as I wait to see whether the magic will activate and enshroud us. For what seems like forever, everyone is silent and waiting with bated breath.

The woman's violet eyes narrow when, finally, the tang of magic blossoms on my tongue.

I can breathe again.

Ancient magic of the land binds certain laws, and Challenges are an example of such magic. When a Challenge is invoked, it must be obeyed to ensure that a ruler does not stay in power for unreasonably long—not when someone else could best them and be a better ruler for the land. I find these rules a little barbaric and animalistic, but most faeries believe it's the only way to keep the semblance of fairness in court monarchy.

She has no choice. She must relent.

Her glossy red lips open to speak, but someone enters, and we turn as one.

A man dressed in fitted, dark blue pants and a tight black shirt strolls into the room, violet eyes flashing with amusement. His hair isn't long, but it's loose.

"Whom am I fighting?" His voice is dark and rough.

One side of Castiel's lips pull up. "No one."

The stranger's eyebrows raise. "Was it your renouncement that I tasted, then?"

"I've invoked a Trial Challenge. Why would I fight a battle I know I'll lose?" Castiel's smirk is a knowing one. He may be arrogant and rude, but he knows when he's outmatched.

Castiel and the new stranger are exact opposites in appearance. Whereas darkness shrouds the stranger, Castiel seems to have a light of his own; the golden strands he's weaved into his clothes sparkle with the bright leaves in his hair.

I don't know who scares me more.

"A Trial Challenge?" The stranger's eyebrows arch even higher. "Those are words I've not heard in a while. Has Euphelia given your trial yet? Hm?" His violet eyes turn to meet identical ones sitting on the throne. "Have you kept our guests waiting?"

If they've heard of the Trial Challenge, they must be much older than I gave them credit for.

Pretty red lips purse. "I was going to call for you, Ryken. I thought you might enjoy coming up with a task... *worthy*... of the Day Prince."

It isn't until I hear both their names that I realize Castiel didn't ask for either of them. He simply strolled in here with me in tow and demanded his way. Not bothering to ask for their names is a show of superiority for which I don't think I'd ever have the confidence. As much as I hate Castiel, I have to admit that I am often envious of his unfounded confidence.

"Ah, so you acknowledge I am still the Prince of Day," Castiel's wry voice echoes in the throne room.

"We've overthrown your court. You are the sole heir. The magic is in our favor..." Euphelia pauses and corrects herself. "*Was* in our favor. Now that you've invoked the Trial, we're bound to see it through. Though, you still have nothing left, so I may as well address you by your title while you still have it." She huffs, as though our intrusion is a mere inconvenience to her day rather than a gamble for the wellbeing of an entire court.

Castiel's back stiffens, but he does not address the taunt. "And what is this worthy Trial you've come up with?"

A dark smile graces Ryken's face, befitting of the murders and crimes he and his sister have committed. "The Forescua Serpent."

Euphelia's eyes dart to her brother and fear flashes across her face for a moment. I blink and it's gone, leaving me to wonder whether I'd imagined it completely.

Castiel's face is free of emotion and he shows no sign of asking, but I've been silent long enough. I'm part of this Trial, and I have a right to know.

"What's the Forescua Serpent?" My voice sounds strange echoing in this chamber—like it knows I don't belong.

Ryken's sharp eyes study me, and I fight to keep my spine straight. "What a shame that such a face has committed herself to death."

I stand my ground and glare. It is not the first time I've had to endure insolence. "I asked a question."

My voice booms this time, and I'm proud it does not quiver in the slightest.

"What's your name?" Euphelia addresses me with narrowed eyes.

"Answer my question, and I'll answer yours." I cross my arms.

Gravelly laughter fills the room, and I struggle to keep my breathing even. "You strike a hard bargain. Fine." Ryken walks up to the broken throne and eases himself onto the armrest, ignoring the purple glare from his sister.

"The Forescua Serpent is one of the oldest creatures from well before the fae split into courts. It is a creature of dark magic. It leaves a trail of death and decay wherever it goes. It is difficult to find, and even harder to kill." Ryken smiles gleefully. "Bring us its head."

Euphelia turns sharply to her brother, but he rests a hand on her shoulder without another word. She regains her composure, and her face is blank once more when she turns to face us.

"Yes," she says haughtily. "Bring us its head, and you shall have your wish. Whatever you desire, you shall have it—even if it is the throne returned to you."

"You will have one week to complete the task," Ryken adds. "Return victorious, and we will leave your court." He pauses, his eyes sliding over to Castiel. "If you so wish."

I suppress a shiver. It's as if he knows.

"Should you fail..." He clicks his tongue. "Well, nothing would matter then, would it? You'd be dead."

CASTIEL AND I STAND in the Courtless fields, out of sight from the other courts. Neither of us has paper or pen, so the fastest way to contact Elysia is to burn a message to her with magic. I turn my palm toward the sky and let the magic flow through me. Letters as large as my head spark to life in the air, forming words as they leave my mouth in whispers.

Burning messages is not a popular method of communication amongst the fae because of the message's literal size. There is no privacy when sending it, nor is there privacy for the receiver; the words are written in giant, emblazoned letters for everyone near the recipient to see.

Meet me in the Courtless, my dark blue flames spell out. I watch as the fire burns itself out and ash drops to the grass in little piles.

"And how is Elysia to know who sent this message?" Castiel's blond brow quirks as he watches a breeze blow some ash away.

"She'll know."

He seems doubtful, but I know my cousin.

Seconds turn into minutes, but Elysia does not keep us waiting. A rift of inky blackness tears in the air before us and through it, my white-haired cousin steps out with our human sister on her arm.

Elysia's hair is in two braids hanging over her shoulders, and she is in light Knight garb. She wears a black high neck shirt which leaves the shoulders and upper arms exposed. Her forearms are wrapped in leather, and a belt rests on her hips, holding a thin sheath with a shining silver handle. She wears short black pants with knee-high leather boots.

Her full warrior gear is much more protective, but she knows the message is from me and has no need for it.

Alfynia separates from Elysia and crosses her arms. Her dark brown hair tumbles in waves over a cream sweater. Her navy skirt ruffles in the wind.

A hand on her hip, Elysia huffs. "What is he still doing here?"

"Maybe you should be more careful when you realmwalk without full gear," he bristles.

"Shut up," I walk past him and pull them both into a hug. Elysia relaxes, and they wrap me in their arms. For a moment, I feel peace.

Until he speaks again.

"What exactly can they do for us?" He drawls.

Elysia stiffens and we separate, glaring at the golden prince and his foul mouth.

"What makes you think we'll help you?" Alfynia crosses her arms again and frowns.

I step between them before they can start a brawl in the middle of the field.

Taking a deep breath, I prepare myself for an inevitable talking-to from my sisters. Elysia narrows her honey-gold eyes at me.

"Castiel has invoked a Challenge by trial, and I've agreed to help him." The words tumble out of my mouth, and for a moment I think she has missed what I've said.

But she sighs at the same time Alfynia furrows her brows. "There are other ways to challenge than through combat?"

"We only just learned that when a monarch or an heir is on the brink of losing his throne, he can invoke either a Challenge by combat or by trial. Those who threaten to depose him will give a quest to be completed within a certain time period, and if successful, the heir can have whatever he wishes," I explain. "Apparently it's something like a last chance to reclaim the throne when you've lost everything."

"You know I love you," Alfynia takes a step from Elysia. "But isn't this something with which Queen Maven could better help?"

"Don't you know anything, *mortal*?" Castiel's drawl makes me roll my eyes to the sky. "Queens and kings cannot interfere in any Challenges."

"Don't talk to her that way," I snap. I wait for him to continue, and I glare when he doesn't. Turning my gaze to Alfynia, I explain patiently. "It's an attempt to prevent Court rulers from monopolizing other courts. Monarchs can send their subjects to Challenge, but then those challengers are on their own."

Alfynia nods. There are certain things about our lives that I forget are not inherent to her; while we are born with instincts of faerie cultures and traditions—pieces of our history born in our blood—as a changeling, she must learn these things as she encounters them.

Elysia and I see and accept her as one of us, but she has troubles feeling confident with her place in Asteria. It pains me to see the hurt on her face when she recognizes these moments as little reminders of how different she is.

"Does that mean you can't use our library, too?" She asks quietly.

I want to punch Castiel in the face for making her feel this way, but I know deep inside, these insecurities and fears are hers and hers alone. There is nothing any of us can do to heal this part of her.

"We can," I answer. "But I called you here so I could ask you first."

To compensate for her lack of inherent knowledge, Alfynia has read more than any faerie; I wouldn't be surprised if someone were to claim she had read every book in their court as well as ours. I nod at my sister. "If anyone can tell me whether the library will be useful, it's you."

Alfynia huffs and uncrosses her arms, shaking out of her self-conscious moment. "Flattery will get you everywhere, won't it?"

"Only when it comes to you," I grin.

"Let's get on with this, shall we?" Castiel's voice rumbles so deep I think I can feel it in the very air around us. He's losing patience.

A part of me is afraid of him and what he will do—but that's silly. What *can* he do? His life now depends on me. His words might hurt me, but I'll survive. If I abandon him, he will lose his life. Whatever this Forescua Serpent is, it will be me who beheads it.

My inner voice chides me. Just because he is barely comparable to anyone in swordsmanship does not mean he is without magic or power; he is also high fae. He may not have the ability to lay waste to a dragon, but he is skilled enough to manipulate someone into doing it for him.

And that makes him more dangerous. I shouldn't forget that.

While I debate internally, I scoff externally.

His blue eyes flash with annoyance until I continue. "Unfortunately, he's right. We only have seven days to complete this task. Have you ever heard of the Forescua Serpent?"

Alfynia's emerald eyes widen, and her jaw drops slightly. She recovers quickly, though. "The... Forescua Serpent?"

"Yes, do you need us to repeat it for you slower this time?" Castiel drawls.

"Are we helping you or not?" Elysia spits at him.

"At this rate, I'm thinking we're better off on our own."

I let out a growl of frustration and swipe my hand in the air, closing it when I complete an arch. Dark blue sparkles jump from my hands and launch at his face. His eyes widen and he ducks—because, while he isn't good with offensive combat, he is, I'll admit, decent with defensive maneuvers—but my magic is faster, and it follows.

His eyes narrow with hatred as he straightens. A band of sparkling midnight blue is wrapped over his lips, covering his mouth like a gag.

It's easy magic—simple enough that even he can get out of the binding without a thought. But he understands my intentions and allows his mouth to be magicked shut.

Elysia doesn't even snicker at the gag—her attention is entirely on Alfynia. Though our mortal sister has undeniable knowledge gaps with certain things about Asteria, her voracious appetite for books means she makes up for it in other ways.

Alfynia licks her lips.

Finally, she speaks, shuddering as she does so. "The Forescua Serpent is an ancient creature. It's one of the legendary Elder Ones from the days before the courts were formed—before even King Eldritch united all the fae groups into the original kingdom. The faerie courts are over two thousand years old, and Eldritch's kingdom lasted two thousand before that. The Elder Ones are said to be even older."

Alfynia clenches her fist as she continues. "It's said to be titanic in size and leaves death and decay wherever it goes. Back when the Eldritch kingdom regularly fought off Elder Ones, the Forescua Serpent was rarely one they fended against until one day... it grew angry and malevolent."

"When most of the Elders were all but sealed when the courts formed, the serpent set its sights on the Lunar Court and wrought destruction whenever it could, bringing as much death as possible. And then, it disappeared as quickly as it turned violent." Alfynia shakes her head, her brown waves cascading. "No one knows why it suddenly got so angry, and no one knows why it suddenly disappeared. Some say that someone in the Lunar Court angered it, and when the Dark fae destroyed the Lunar Court, the serpent saw no more need for revenge. Some say the serpent was so angry that the trigger must have been familial—perhaps a Lunar faerie stole one of its eggs or something."

Panic bubbles at my throat, but I swallow it. I don't want any of them to know how nervous I truly feel. "Is there... is there anything in the library that can help us locate this serpent?"

My stomach grows heavy with dread when she shakes her head. "I've studied Elders for a long time, but there's nothing there that can help you with finding it. There's hardly any information about them at all. Besides, if you only have one week to finish this task, there's no time to waste poring over books."

I twist my fingers in my hands.

Alfynia looks over at me with the unmistakable weight of sadness in her gaze. Even Castiel is quiet.

"What do we do?" I whisper.

"There has to be something," Elysia says. She and I have our gaze turned to Alfynia, but I can't help but notice in my periphery that Castiel is looking the other way.

Even now, when his own life hangs on the line, he refuses to turn to a mortal for help.

How pathetic.

Alfynia reaches over and takes my hand in hers; hers are warm and, unlike mine, soft and uncalloused. Where Elysia and I are fighters, Alfynia is a reader. I suspect, with pain in my heart, that she tries to make up for her mortality through knowledge and learning. It must have hurt her an unimaginable amount when Castiel pointed out something she did not know—something inherent to us fae.

Again, I want to wrap my hands around his neck and shake it until his head pops off.

"You have to summon the Vorukael," Alfynia's hands tighten around mine, but it's as if they're tightening around my throat, instead.

"You want us to summon an Elder One so we can get information on how to catch another Elder One?" Castiel scoffs.

I close my eyes. "I see you're talking again."

"Seriously, this mortal wants us to get an Elder involved?"

"This mortal is my *sister*," I hiss.

"What better way to find an Elder than by getting the inside information from another Elder?" Elysia nods. "That could work."

I suppress a shiver.

"How do you suppose?" He sneers.

"Of the Elder Ones that aren't sealed, the Vorukael is the most active and also the least malevolent," I explain. "It only pops up occasionally to cause mischief and mayhem, rather than actual violence. You didn't do very well at the Academy, did you?"

Blue eyes darken and narrow, and I struggle to keep my breathing even.

"You know what I did at the Academy."

I know exactly what he spent his time on. No one could have imagined he'd be the sole heir to the Day Court, so he spent his time lounging and having fun, ignoring his studies and his practice.

Tormenting his peers as he saw fit.

"And look where it got us," I hiss.

A dark grin pulls lazily across his face. "Right next to you, it appears."

I groan and look to the sky for patience. Why am I cursed to be so weak that I couldn't leave him to die?

"Do you even want to win this Challenge?" I glare at him.

He shrugs. "The land demands that I do. And if we don't, then I'd be too dead to care."

I close my eyes. He might not care much about winning, but I need him to win. I'm not excited for a life of queenship, and renouncing it isn't an option—how could I bring such shame to my mother when she had achieved all that she had only for her one child to renounce?

No. We have to win. Leaving my throne so I could take a position at another court is the only way I can stay out of the spotlight. The only way to escape a position I don't even deserve.

It's the only way.

And if he doesn't care enough to help? Well, I don't need him. As long as he stays out of my way, I can win this for the both of us.

"You guys should stay home. Make sure that the wards are fortified, and that mother is prepared. There hasn't been a Dark fae attack on our court since she came into power, but I fear she may be too stubborn to work with other courts even to protect ourselves from them. Just in case."

Elysia nods somberly.

"And you?" Alfynia asks, one hand fiddling with the rowan necklace that's safely situated on her neck once again.

"I'm going hunting for the Vorukael."

CHAPTER FIVE

"WHERE ARE WE?" I ASK, sweating in the afternoon sun.

I have been following Castiel into the Courtless for hours, and my feet ache.

"You said the Vorukael likes secluded spots." He squints against the sun and heads toward another hill for us to climb.

"Why couldn't we have realmwalked?"

"Because you can't realmwalk somewhere you've never been, can you?" He smirks.

"No," I mutter under my breath. "But clearly *you've* been there." Faeries can only realmwalk to places they've been, which means he could have brought us both there instead of making me suffer with all this walking.

He stills. He hasn't broken a sweat despite the hot summer sun beating down on us, and his hair ruffles loosely in the wind. His face is devoid of all emotion when he speaks. "I can't."

"What do you mean you can't?" I ask, my voice almost shrill with fatigue. "You did it before."

"No," he crosses his arms and breathes out heavily through his nose. "You did it. I just rode along."

"What—that—" I pause. "Same thing."

A blond brow arches. "Not the same thing, flower." I bristle as he turns and continues his trek up the grassy hill. "Just a little more and we should be far enough from the courts for you to summon it."

"How do you know these parts of the land, anyway?" I grumble. Faeries tend to avoid the Courtless unless there's an inexplicably good reason to venture in. It is filled with natural magic that feels wild and foreign to us—and if faeries hate anything, it is something with which we are unfamiliar.

Once faeries have fulfilled the graduation requirements with the mandatory trip out to the Courtless, most only come out for official court meetings with the other monarchs—and even then, they send representatives in their places whenever possible.

For Castiel to be so familiar with the Courtless lands was odd.

"I used to explore," he shrugs.

My eyes narrow. "You explored?"

"Yes."

"You explored the Courtless?" I repeat.

"Yes," he sighs and rubs the back of his neck. "We don't all have sisters to run home to."

"You have—had—seven siblings." I stumble with my correction, but he doesn't acknowledge it, and I'm grateful.

"Siblings mean nothing if they don't care for you." He stops at the top of a cliff and checks the surrounding area. Satisfied, he nods. "Is this good enough for you?"

I bite the question at the tip of my tongue—I don't need to learn about his personal family issues in order to win this for us—and look around.

The skies are cloudless and blue. The cliff we stand on is not small like I originally thought—in fact, a quick tumble would cause some serious damage even to a high faerie. A few trees scatter along the edge, and over it, sharp jagged rocks stare ominously back at me.

I nod.

"What do you need?" He's looking at me with those earnest blue eyes—so bright and blue they're almost clear—and I feel like I can't breathe.

It's hard to remember he's cruel when he looks the way he does.

I hate it.

He tilts his head and is about to speak when I interrupt—I don't think I could endure the teasing if he realizes I was thinking about his eyes rather than about strangling him.

"The Vorukael is a trickster; he loves mischief and mayhem," I think out loud. "But he also can't lie, which means he loves to think of ways to twist the truth. He's rarely seen, but when he is, the scandal has already begun—he smells the scent of mischief and shows up to make things worse for his own entertainment."

Castiel is still for a strangely long time before finally speaking. "I have an idea to make him show up if you know how to trap him."

"I—"

"Or are you not going to be pulling your weight around here?"

"Trapping him isn't the hard part," I snap. "What's your idea?"

His brows arch and one side of his lips pull up. "You worry about your part, and I'll worry about mine."

"This isn't—" I sputter. "How do I know you'll do your part correctly?"

"We'll find out, won't we?"

He wanders downhill and out of my sight. I huff and cross my arms.

Then, I uncross them because pouting will not get me anywhere.

First, I conjure a circle of ash. Atop the ash, I lay links of silver and iron. The Elder Ones are some of the oldest faeries known to us, and as such, they have a weakness to both silver and iron, whereas the same weakness has been bred out from us over the generations.

Finally, as Castiel strolls back, I conjure and place the rowan branches last. Faeries can't actually create much with magic. We can borrow, replace, and temporarily make the corporeal form of many things, but things to which we have natural weakness—like rowan or oak—we cannot truly create. The same goes for food; we can create food with magic, but it doesn't taste very good, and it doesn't sustain us either.

"What's your big idea? We'd better start because these branches will disappear in about five minutes." I wave my hand at the circle I've created.

He smirks darkly. Castiel spreads his right arm and lets golden sparks dance along his palm until a bow almost the length of his body blinks into existence. In his left, the same magic twirls along his hand, resting at his wrist, until a quiver appears.

My heart races and I take a step back, nearly stepping on the rowan branches.

"What are you—"

"Relax," he rolls his eyes. "I'm not going to shoot you."

"I—of course you're not." I ease the tension out of my voice and hope that I sound confident—haughty, even, like him. "I just meant—what are you doing with that?"

"Nothing." He holds both so they lay horizontally in front of him. Castiel crosses the distance between us and pushes the bow and arrows toward me. "You're going to use them."

The bow is a lovely shade of dark brown—the color of bark wetted by a heavy rain. Golden strands are weaved throughout, depicting symbols of the sun, of light, and of life. Ancient runes are delicately inscribed in gold—a language I cannot understand—and it's all I can do not to gasp at its beauty.

"What am I supposed to do with this?"

"Shoot me," he grins. It's a toothy smile, and I can't decide if he's joking.

"Excuse me?"

Castiel smirks, placing the bow and arrows in my hand; they're lighter than I expected.

"You're going to shoot me with it. Light it up. Shoot me." He takes a step back and puts both hands on my arms just below the shoulders. Heat seeps through my sleeves and I can feel the warmth of his hands on my skin as he slowly switches our places until he stands in front of the circle.

My mouth opens and I have no words as I watch him step back, stopping only when he's in the middle of the iron and rowan trap.

He drops his hands to his sides. His head lolls, the cheeky grin still present on his smug face. "Come on. You know you've been wanting to do this."

A bow this big should not be so light in my hands, so it must be ancient—forged before the methods of creating this type of weaponry was lost to us. How does he possess such an item? Why?

It thrums in my hands as if it can read my thoughts.

It doesn't matter why Castiel owns such a treasure. All that matters is that he's right. Shooting him would finally fulfil a fantasy I'd only dreamed of for so long.

"What?" I can't bring my gaze to meet his because he knows he is right.

"Are you incapable of lighting the arrow? I thought you were the best warrior of our year."

"I was the best *swordsman*," I correct him. "I'm only decent with a bow."

The annoying smirk is on his face again. With his back against the cliff and the sun, he has that odd glow that I've only seen from Day faeries. Only, I don't think I've ever seen it so strong with anyone else, and it's infuriating.

"You're the best in our year. The best our generation has seen. Don't be modest."

A breeze caresses my cheek, like the wind itself is agreeing with him. Like Castiel's persuasive charm is so strong, even the wild nature herself cannot disagree.

"I just don't know why you're telling me to shoot you. This hardly seems scandalous enough for the Vorukael to appear. It's not the first time courts have threatened each other."

"Trust me."

My eyes narrow. "Why should I?"

"You're here, aren't you?" His head tilts, a strange sparkle in his light blue eyes.

"I swear to Sirona, if you die..." I growl under my breath. He only arches his eyebrows and raises his hands, palms facing me.

Taunting me.

Taking a deep breath to steady my heart, I close my eyes. My hands know the motions, but they still test the bow. My right thumb and index finger roll the slender arrow; my other hand flexes against the unfamiliar wood, letting it speak to me.

I listen.

My back straightens as my muscles wake to remember the motions. I breathe out. The arrow is nocked.

The bow is drawn.

I aim.

I let out a breath and loose the arrow.

A flash of fear wraps around my heart, but I light the arrow up, anyway. My magic twirls around the thin piece of wood, coating the tip and fortifying it. It glows midnight blue as it sprints eagerly toward Castiel's heart.

An involuntary shout leaps from my throat as I watch the deadly arrow approach its prey in slow motion.

At the last second, a plume of black smoke appears like a wall in front of Castiel, protecting him from his own arrow.

It drops uselessly to the ground, blue magic extinguished.

Blood pounds in my ears as I watch the smoke settle, blinking out of existence in wisps.

My throat tightens and dread pools in my stomach.

The Vorukael has appeared.

And it holds Castiel by the throat.

CHAPTER SIX

THE VORUKAEL IS SMALL for an Elder One; he's about the same height and size as Castiel, though he dangles Castiel in the air like the princeling weighs nothing. He wears a long, tattered robe which does not touch the ground—beneath it, I see no feet. He seems to glide in the air, little wisps of inky smoke curling from the grass to reach for the bottom of his grey cloak.

I realize with horror that beneath his hood, there is no face. Instead, I see darkness—a void—where his face should be, though obsidian eyes sparkling with mischief stare at Castiel with wonder, ignoring me completely.

Castiel stares right back into those ebony eyes. He does not flinch as long, pointed nails dig into his skin. He does not seem afraid as the gnarled fingers of the Vorukael tighten around his throat.

But I am.

If he dies, no one else will take me—no one is as stupid or desperate as he. He's my only way out of the throne. Out from somewhere I don't belong.

Castiel has the audacity to smirk, and I want to hiss at him to stop when he speaks.

"Welcome," Castiel rasps. "Beautiful day, isn't it?"

Shut up. Shut up. Shut—

"A *delicious* day," a voice responds, and my spine stiffens. I can't tell if the voice is in my head or all around us, but I hear the sighs of a thousand fae behind it, reminiscent of the lost fae we encounter when realmwalking.

I shudder and tighten my grip on the bow, though I have a feeling that even if Castiel's bow were made of old magic, the weapon is useless against this Elder.

"What is it you've summoned me for, little faeries?" The voice addresses us both, but his beady gaze is still on Castiel, who's dangling and struggling for breath. Those dark stones for eyes sparkle as they study his face.

"Let him down and we can talk." I'm proud that my voice does not tremble, though it's nowhere near the level I want it to be.

His head turns to me in an instant. It's like he's stolen my breath when his gaze meets mine.

He makes an odd tinkling sound—almost like he's laughing at me—and tilts his faceless head. The hood droops with the motion, though never falling off.

"Are you in any position to be making demands?" A thousand more voices have joined, making it creepier and more ethereal.

"It was a request. A humble one," I say through gritted teeth. I force my arm to lower so he can see I pose no threat—though the thought I am a threat to such an ancient and powerful being is laughable.

The odd laughing sound fills the air and my mind again. Bubbles of panic rise in my throat as I watch Castiel's smirk slip when his *stupid* body dangles *uselessly* in the air.

Faster than my eyes can discern, the Vorukael flicks his arm and Castiel flies toward me—he's *thrown* the princeling like a doll, winding me when his body collides with mine, sending us tumbling in the grass.

I thank Sirona that we positioned the circle by the cliff, because we roll roughly down the grassy hills instead of tumbling into open air and toward uncertain death.

Grunting with pain, I shove him off and we recover quickly. I curl my hands into fists as anger builds in my chest with each step toward the Vorukael, who hovers within the iron circle.

"What was that for?" I breathe heavily, trying to remember whom I'm facing. Even within the iron, silver, and rowan circlet, he's not powerless. I would do well to remember it.

With a flick of my wrist behind my back, I conjure more rowan branches to the circle just in case the first ones have run out of time.

Though he has no face, I swear his inky eyes glint with amusement.

"You have your prince of sun and light," the voices intertwined with his seem to tinkle as he speaks. "Now, what is it you seek?"

I don't bother correcting the Vorukael; Castiel is not *my* prince, but this isn't the time or place.

"We're on a Challenge by trial," Castiel drawls from behind me. His bow is nowhere in sight. "And we're to hunt the Forescua Serpent."

The Vorukael pauses for a moment, bringing a gnarled finger to where his chin would have been if he had one.

"So, I suppose you wish to know how to find it, and then how to kill it?"

"I *suppose* that would be helpful," Castiel responds.

"He doesn't mean to be so sarcastic," I rush to speak before Castiel can anger the ancient faerie. "He needs a lesson—or ten—in manners."

The same ominous tinkle, not unlike a chime, fills the air again and for a moment, I am confused.

Then I realize he's laughing. The Vorukael is *laughing*.

I don't know whether to feel happy or insulted.

"As you may well know," he speaks as his shiny, dark pebbles for eyes dart back and forth between us. "I cannot speak a lie, so I can tell you what you wish to know."

He pauses dramatically, and I resist rolling my eyes to the sky.

"However, I do not give information for free."

"What is it you want?" I ask a little too enthusiastically—perhaps foolishly so. He might have figured we were eager for this information before, but now he definitely knows that we are desperate.

"What I require is not difficult in a physical sense." He puts together the tips of his gnarled fingers. Dread pools in my stomach the longer the pause drags on.

"All I require..." The wind chime laughter fills the air again. "Is a secret."

I blink.

"A... secret?" I ask, unsure if I've heard correctly. Beside me, Castiel stiffens.

"Yes."

"You mean like... court secrets?" I rack my brain for something that I could share with an Elder without catastrophically endangering my court.

"No," he responds gleefully. "A secret of *your own*. One that you've told no one else. Something you can hardly stomach to admit even to yourself."

Voice stuck in my throat, I don't know what to say. Does he want me to admit how weak I feel? How afraid I am of being a queen? How utterly unfit it is for a halfling like me to have a stake to the Night throne?

As if he's read my mind, he speaks again. "Something you hate about yourself. Something you wish was not true, but you also cannot help. Something that is a part of you—of your very *essence*."

"I'm afraid to be queen." I hear my words echo in the chasms below and cringe. I'd never admitted it to anyone before—not even Elysia and Alfynia—but I am afraid. I am terrified, and I can feel deep in my soul that I'm not meant to be the Night Queen.

Fear rules me, and I am weak because of it. I would not make a good Queen of the Night Court. Of this, I am sure.

"Not that," he hisses. I'm confused because he's also... laughing?

I flinch at first but stop when I realize that his voice comprises of a thousand *gaily* fae.

He's enjoying this. I grit my teeth and clench my hands, but refrain from throwing a rude gesture at him.

"What... what more do you want?"

Castiel breathes hard beside me. His hands have curled into fists—knuckles white—and his eyes are locked on the ground, seeing something I cannot.

The excited whispers of countless fae fill the air around us as a cool wind plays with our hair. As if those invisible fae are the ones toying with us.

My heart hammers. I try to figure out what Castiel already knows.

Finally, he makes a noise like a croak and looks up.

He clears his throat, and his chin is high as he stares down those obsidian pebbles shining blithely.

"I am obsessed with Astrid."

My jaw drops. My heart stops.

I blink hard, tempted to rub my eyes or clear out my ears. Something is wrong.

Someone is playing a trick on us—on me. This can't be real.

"I have been since the day I heard her name and who she is," he continues. His blue eyes are trained on the Vorukael and his smoky shadows. Castiel refuses to look at me, even as I stare at him with disbelief. "It only got worse when I saw her for the first time."

"What?"

They both ignore me. The Vorukael looks at him expectantly, waiting for more. Gleeful.

"It might be love, but I'm not sure. I don't know what love is or what it's like. I know enough about obsession to recognize I am obsessed with her. Against my every wish, against my own logic and mind, against every fiber of my being, I am deeply and wildly obsessed with Astrid Vanaguard."

I swallow hard.

He stays as still as a statue except for his clenched jaw, which he works, even as he continues to stare at the Vorukael. The wind-chime-laughter grows louder.

I see it in Castiel's stance. I see it in the way his muscles coil with tension, the way he can barely contain the shaking of his fists, curled at his side.

He hates this.

He hates this feeling he harbors for me, and he hates admitting it out loud, especially in front of me.

He hates me.

This is not easy for him to admit, nor is it easy for me to hear.

But that is precisely why the Vorukael makes him say it. He blithely soaks in the tension and confusion in the air, breathing it in like sustenance.

"Ah, *delicious* day." He has no mouth, but I know he's smiling at us.

"Will you tell us what we seek?" Castiel growls through gritted teeth. I can almost feel the reverberations in my chest.

"I shall," he pauses. "And for that utterly scrumptious secret, I will give you a little more, too." I must be mistaken, because I think he *winks* at us. How is that even possible?

"The Forescua Serpent has made its home in the darkest part of the moonlit lands. It has been there for centuries and has no desire to move. It lives not in a cave or a tunnel, but in the open forest. It can be hard to find, but you'll know when you see it."

"And how do we kill it?" I ask. While the Vorukael tilts its head to me, Castiel does not move.

"That part may be a little difficult for you. The serpent has incomparable regenerative abilities; you cut off its head, and it shall grow two more. To prevent that from happening, you'll need a healthy dose of everfyre. Light up your fancy sword in the blue flames, and the Forescua's body will be no more."

"I've heard of everfyre..." Castiel finally speaks again, though his voice sounds rough. "It's Lunar magic."

The Vorukael nods. "I'm sure that between the two of you, you'll figure out how to get it from deep within the Lunar caves of old. You'll find all that you need in the oldest moon-bleached forest."

"How do we get there?" I ask. My voice is a little hoarse, too. This challenge is sounding more difficult by the minute.

The air fills with windchimes. "Child, your secret was not that good. You'll have to do some work yourselves. But worry not..." His inky eyes lock onto my gaze, and I freeze. "*You'll know.*"

Black smoke rises from the ground and engulfs the Vorukael entirely in a whirlwind of dark shadows. Wind whips us as thunder sounds in my ears.

As he disappears, whispers fill the air. "And one more thing... the everfyre will get you to the everfyre."

What?

I blink hard against the rising smoke and shadows as I prepare to raise a shield against the small rocks, ash, and silver and iron chains that are sent flying.

When the air calms, the Vorukael is gone.

I lower the protection spell and I see Castiel staring at me with raw hatred in his deep blue eyes.

CHAPTER SEVEN

"THE VORUKAEL COULD have left the circle this entire time?" He growls, eyes shining with raw hatred and... something else. Something I don't want to explore.

I start taking a step back from the ferocity of his stare, but I stop.

Why am I backing away from him? His life depends on me. I have no need to fear him.

"No," I answer calmly. "The rowan branches must have disappeared without either of us noticing. This encounter took longer than we anticipated."

He looks away, breathing hard. Hands curled into fists at his side.

The sun starts to set, but it only serves to make him more beautiful, casting glows and shadows in all the right places. His cheekbones are high, and his jaw is so sharp I wonder if my hands would bleed if I were to run them down his face. What a silly, stupid thought to have.

His obsession worries me. It's not a complication we need in a time like this—or ever.

"Forget what you heard," he finally rasps. His eyes, darkening with the setting sun, turn to me and he holds my gaze. The shadows of his clenched jaw flicker.

I think I've forgotten how to breathe.

"It's not something I'm happy with, but neither is it something I can change. Sirona knows I've tried. I have no desire to act upon it, or for our situation to be anything else other than what it is now. So," he takes a deep breath. "Just forget what you heard. I said it so we could move on with the Challenge, and it worked."

I didn't understand why shooting Castiel with his own bow and arrow would summon the Vorukael, but I understand now.

It was because of the princeling's secret obsession with me.

The Vorukael wasn't interested in warring courts—he enjoyed the misery, tension, and chaos he caused between two faeries working together.

Not just any two faeries.

Two enemies driven by hatred of each other.

Two absolute opposites.

On top of it all, he forced Castiel to admit something neither of us wanted—or needed—to hear.

I bite my lip. For the first time, I notice his eyes dart to my mouth before flickering back up to my eyes. I stop worrying my lip and sigh deeply.

"You're right. You said it out of necessity. I still hate you, and you still hate me. We need each other right now, but nothing needs to change."

His shoulders sag with relief before he straightens, that haughty and arrogant look back on his face. The air of confidence simmering around him like the glow of the setting sun.

Neither of us are in the mood to speak, but we share a mutual understanding to start making our way to the Lunar Court.

I can't help but wonder whether he is relieved that I agreed not to give him grief about his feelings, or if his relief is from finally having admitted out loud the secret he'd harbored for so long.

THE NEXT DAY, WE DON'T mention the Vorukael as we walk side-by-side past the outskirts of a forest toward the land that used to be the Lunar Court.

Unlike the curated ones in our courts, the Courtless forests are large, wild, and unruly. I have seen several trees as high as mountains, their tips disappearing into the clouds. Sustained by the natural magic of Asteria, underbrush sprawls all around us so that it feels as though we're deep in an unknown jungle rather than in the woods of the neutral land.

"Remind me why you can't realmwalk," I say casually.

"I didn't tell you to begin with," he casts a sideways glance.

His hair is unruly today, as if feeding on the wild magic like the forest flora. I watched earlier in the morning as he pulled his hand through the golden locks several times until, frustrated, he dismissed the mirror and gave up.

It looks better this way, I think secretly to myself.

With his hair loose, bits of it over his forehead instead of pushed back, he looks younger. Kinder.

I almost snort when I think of him as *kind*.

Castiel Ares is not kind.

He's overconfident, cruel, and too charming for his own good.

"But since you're subjecting me to walk so much, I think I'm entitled to know." I stop and cross my arms.

It takes several paces before he pauses and realizes I am not next to him.

He sighs heavily and looks up to the skies, as if lightning could just strike him down now instead of having to deal with me.

I smirk, knowing he can't get out of this one.

"What if I made it so you wouldn't have to walk?" He asks, reluctantly bringing his gaze to mine.

Today, his eyes are a deeper blue than usual. It's unsettling that I notice the changes in his eyes. Even at the Academy, I'd noticed how his eyes changed color whenever I had the misfortune of running into him. Even as cruel as he was—as I know he still is—I'm not immune to his good looks.

And I feel shallow for it.

"How is that possible?" I tilt my head in question. I still want to know why he can't realmwalk, but I'm curious to find out what he can come up with instead.

He looks at me warily for a moment, as if second guessing whether he should reveal whatever he's about to tell. Just as I'm about to tell him off for such a weak lie, he purses his lips and releases a whistle so unnaturally loud and shrill that birds take to the skies.

"What the—?" I stumble backward and nearly trip when, through the thick tree trunks, a shadowy rip appears in the fabric of the air.

The echo of a howl fills my ears.

A giant black blur bursts out.

I gasp and my heart races to my throat when the blur jumps in between me and Castiel, lunging for him.

Instinct takes over and I throw my hand up. Magic crackles on my fingertips, and a dark blue shield raises in front of the princeling. The mammoth of black fur collides with it and bounces back in a flash of sparks, whimpering in pain before turning on me.

Rows of teeth longer than my fingers are visible in its open maw. Silver eyes glare at me as a growl rumbles deep in its chest. It crouches on all fours, ready to pounce.

It's a *wolf*.

A giant, pure black wolf with silver eyes. It stands a little taller than me. Its paws are huge and heavy, but it makes no sound as it advances; each step is calculated.

Silent like the predator I know it is.

I let out a sound of fear and clench my fist. Nails dig into my palm. Magic gathers in my hands, aching under my skin. I let out a shuddering breath and am about to speak a spell when Castiel's voice pierces through the fog of tension between me and the dangerous mountain of fur and teeth.

"Rowan!"

I blink with disbelief as the giant wolf tilts its head and stops advancing. It closes its jaw and sits on its haunches, looking back at Castiel. It lets out a low whine.

Its giant tail thumps against the ground, sending little waves of vibration up the soles of my feet.

Castiel walks up to the wolf and takes its head in his hands before I can utter a cry of protest. He presses his forehead against the wolf's head, and they stay like that for several moments while I am rooted in my spot.

What is happening?

Castiel steps back from the wolf and gives me a wry smile.

"This is Rowan. He won't harm you."

"*He*?" I am vaguely aware that my voice has reached new levels of shrill. "*Rowan*?"

"Yes. We're friends." The wolf sits quietly next to Castiel, his head tilting one way and then another, intelligent silver eyes studying me. Castiel's hand is lost in its fur.

"How? You?" I look back and forth between the golden faerie and the black wolf, sputtering.

He swallows hard and his arm flexes as he digs his hand deeper into Rowan's fur. "Yes, I can talk to animals. Rowan has been my friend for many years. I found him when I was a child and he was a pup, and I raised him out here."

"But—"

"I know," he glowers. "Talking with animals is a lesser fae trait, so my family forced me to hide this shameful skill of mine." He tilts his head. "But I suppose it isn't a problem anymore, is it?"

My cheeks flush with warmth. "I didn't mean to insinuate..."

He waves me off. "It is of no concern to me. I know how we high fae think of lesser fae and their skills."

"No," I stop him, struggling to find the words. "I don't harbor any judgement. This... this is pretty cool."

He doesn't look as if he believes me, but he doesn't argue further.

"Can I pet him?" My hands are against my chest, and I take a tentative step forward.

"He doesn't mind," Castiel removes his hand from Rowan's fur and takes a step back, giving me space as I approach.

"Hi," I whisper. I put my hand out, but let it hover in the air. "I'm sorry about the shield. Are you okay?"

Castiel's dark chuckle fills my ears and I want to turn and glare at him, but I keep my eyes trained on the wolf in front of me. Nerves dance under my skin and I'm afraid even to breathe as Rowan studies my hand for a moment before pushing against it.

I gasp when I get a handful of his fur. It's softer than I expect, but what surprises me most is the magic I feel emanating from his body. No other animal exudes power and intelligence like that which I feel from Rowan.

"What are you?" I breathe.

"He's from the Other Realm," Castiel answers. I'm so engrossed with Rowan that I don't even notice when he approaches to stand beside me.

The love and care in his eyes as he gazes upon his wolf is unlike anything I'd ever seen from him—a look I never thought would grace the cruel prince's face. This wolf is a lot more than just a friend to Castiel; I suspect the wolf is closer to family for the golden prince than his own family ever was.

"I think he followed someone out of the Other Realm or something while he was still too young to take care of himself. I was wandering the woods when I found him crying under a young rowan tree."

"Hence the name," I say, still marveling at the silky black tufts between my fingers. It's a fitting name. As I run my hand down his mane-like fur, I know deep in my heart that this other worldly being should be feared by the fae, just as his namesake is. "I didn't even know there were other creatures in the Other Realm."

He nods. "There's a lot we aren't taught. He's a little different from normal wolves, so he hasn't been able to find a pack of his own. He's made a few friends, but I think I'm his pack."

They're each other's pack, a voice whispers in the corner of my mind—a realization that I was right. This wolf is his family.

I'm silent as I listen to his voice, which sounds oddly soothing when he's explaining about something he loves. It's a drastic difference from when he's insulting or being sarcastic. It's almost calming and pleasant.

"You asked before why I spent so much time out here." His voice is quiet as his eyes trace the wolf's body. "These days, it's mostly because of Rowan. But even before I met him, I used to spend a lot of time out here because there's no judgement from the animals."

He chuckles. "Or at least, the judgement out here is not quite the same as from the other fae. Plus, it's the only way I can talk to the animals without someone realizing what I can do."

I wonder what the animals say. I wonder how their judgement and their thoughts differ from the fae.

For a moment, I think I understand Castiel a little more. He is—was—the youngest of eight children. In Asteria, we consider the number seven to be lucky. We all heard the rumors when the Day Queen was with child again. Everyone said misfortune would befall the family because of him.

I suppose they were right.

As the youngest with no chance at the throne, his people didn't care about him. His siblings were cruel, refusing to acknowledge him as part of their family. His own parents neglected him like he was misfortune itself.

And now, learning that they taught him to be ashamed of this skill and forced him to hide it, I understand a little better how he became the person he is today.

Taught to hate a part of himself that only *slightly* resembles traits of the lesser fae—lesser fae can sometimes sense or understand the needs of animals better than we can—it makes sense he would project that prejudice to me when I am half-human. When I'm *less* than lesser fae.

Not that it excuses him of everything he's done, but I can see how it all came to be.

"What makes him different from regular wolves?" I retract my hand and immediately miss the warmth. I want Castiel to confirm my suspicions about this majestic creature.

"You might have noticed he's a little bigger than most," Castiel looks up at Rowan, and something happens when blue meets silver. A type of understanding I can't quite recognize sparks between them—a type of magic with which I'm not familiar.

"He realmwalks, but somehow is always within calling range. I think he has magic of his own, but I don't think he uses it the same way we do. It looks to be more inherent natural magic, though I'm not entirely sure what that even looks like. And he has a pretty good understanding of what we're saying."

The love and pride in that navy gaze shocks me to my very core. Until this moment, I didn't realize he was capable of this.

He says he doesn't know what love is or how it feels, but I think he doesn't realize what he feels for Rowan is pure and unconditional love.

What happens next is so odd that I can barely comprehend it.

He whispers something to Rowan, who then turns and disappears into a black rift that opens in the air.

"He'll be back with a friend," Castiel explains. The stony mask is back on his face, but either I've grown used to his general indifference and sneers, or he's a little less prickly. Maybe he's a little changed after voluntarily sharing this part of himself with me.

"We'll ride to the Lunar lands."

CHAPTER EIGHT

I SQUINT AGAINST THE wind whipping against my face and duck my head closer to the fur beneath me. Castiel says wolves like to run through the forests rather than open plains, so our surrounding land is little more than a blur of greens, browns, and blues as we whip across the Courtless woodlands.

Castiel rides Rowan while I am on the back of a smaller, brown furred wolf. I'm told my mount is a regular nameless wolf, but in my mind, I've taken to calling her Oak because of her fur.

We've been riding for a few hours now, and it's still inconceivable to me that I'm riding a wolf.

Though, I'm not sure if riding is any better than walking—faster, yes, but I quickly realized my body is not used to the ride as it fatigues faster than I expected, even with the odd saddle Castiel conjured.

I squeeze my aching thighs together in the way Castiel taught me to do when I want to stop. It's a little different from riding a horse, but the fundamentals are the same if I ignore the lack of bridle and reins and everything else common to horseback riding. Now that I think about it, the only thing familiar is the way I hold myself—and even that feels strange.

My core aches. My shoulders ache. My hands are numb.

My wolf's head turns slightly, and she lets out a snort before slowing. The thumps of her paws against the ground soften until finally, we're still.

Breathing out heavily, I realize my fingers are still wrapped around the front of my strange saddle, and my jaw aches from having clenched my teeth for so long.

Castiel casually hops off Rowan and gives me a quizzical look.

"Give me a moment," I say through gritted teeth.

I focus on slowing my breathing, then carefully peel my fingers from the saddle. Oak tosses her nose impatiently.

"Sorry," I mumble to the wolf. "This is a little new for me."

When I've finally relaxed my muscles, I slide off my wolf's side with great effort, groaning as I do.

"New to this?" Castiel grins.

"You know I am," I growl back. "Few have the pleasure of saying they're experienced *wolf* riders."

He shrugs. "I figured you were familiar with horseback riding. This isn't much different."

"You remember that not only were you a better rider than I at the Academy, but it has also been many months since I've last ridden—not to mention this is a *little* different from a horse." I glare at him before turning back to Oak. Her honey eyes stare at a nearby bush, unaware of our conversation.

We've stopped, I assume, in the middle of the forest. The ground is uneven beneath my feet, and I marvel at how swiftly the pair of wolves have traveled—and quietly, too. Perfect apex predators.

While Oak pants, Rowan is not out of breath at all.

As Castiel creates a dip in the ground for water, I can't help but notice he is not out of breath, either.

I, on the other hand, am sitting on the ground indignantly stretching my poor aching legs and rolling out my shoulders. I cannot imagine how often—and for how long—he must ride Rowan to be *this* accustomed to riding wolf-back.

A shadow looms and I look up to see pale blue eyes.

He pushes back his hair to no avail—the wind has not been kind to his unruly locks—and crouches in front of me. I lean back as he invades my personal space.

"What are you doing?" I glower when he hovers a hand over my outstretched leg.

"Relax," he chides. "I'm going to fix your aches."

My eyes narrow. "Why?"

He gives me a pointed look. "As I recall, healing was another skill at which you were not so great while at the Academy."

"So, you do recall *some* things from this time," I grumble. "I can do it myself."

"Not if we want to keep going, you can't." He brushes my hand away, and a flash of orange and red fire coats his outstretched fingers. Despite myself, I flinch. He pretends to not notice as the golden glow jumps from his hand to my leg, warming as it reaches me.

I clamp my mouth shut because I know he's right; I am not good at healing magic. Mine is more explosive—not fit for the intricacies required to fix a body.

The warmth spreads from one leg to another and then up to my core. My muscles involuntarily uncoil and relax. He's good at this.

Most fae can perform basic healing—but only on themselves—because healing yourself is easier than healing others when you can feel exactly what's wrong with your body. Those with formal training as healers can mend most injuries, but the mark of a skilled healer is being able to heal others without pain and without scars.

That I feel nothing but warmth and relaxation from Castiel's fingertips is a testament to his abilities.

He continues to shock me.

Back when we were students of the Academy, I had learned to read him and recognize his capabilities so I could better avoid him; I never noticed that he displayed any memorable skill with healing magic, which means he must have hidden the skill well.

Why would he hide this? Why let everyone think he is carefree and untalented?

Maybe his family taught him to be ashamed. Based on what he's revealed, it seems plausible for the Ares family to view healer magic as weak magic—which isn't true at all. It is extremely difficult to weave a faerie's powers delicately enough to repair flesh, muscle, and bone, requiring an enormous amount of patience and skill on top of years of practice. Skilled healers are generally revered, but I can imagine that some condemn the skill as weak because it's not offensive magic.

I suppose I shouldn't be surprised at this hidden talent of his. After all, Castiel has an impressive ability to entwine his magic into persuasive words—not unlike the intricacies of healing a body.

It is unnerving that each new piece of information I glean about him takes him further from the bully I used to know.

"There." Castiel stands up and returns to the wolves, leaving me to test my fresh muscles alone. He doesn't look me in the eye, nor does he ask for gratitude.

"Why didn't I know you were good at healing?"

His back stiffens slightly, but the smirk is already in place when he turns around.

"Why do you ask?"

"As *I* recall, you didn't particularly excel in any department." I hold his gaze, unabashed to tell the truth of his lacking skills. "But you seem quite adept at this."

"There is no esteem in being good at supportive magic, just as there is none in talking to animals," he looks at me pointedly. "Think about who my family was and what their powers were." Castiel tilts his head.

"Just because your magic works differently from theirs, you hide it?"

He shakes his head, sandy hair bouncing slightly. "There is no pride in my magic."

I see the resolve in his eyes and I swallow my reply. My mother never made me feel hated or ashamed because I am a halfling. She tells me that there is greatness in being human—that humanity makes me different from the other fae *in a good way*, and that it is my human side which will make me a better ruler one day than she ever could be.

I don't believe her, but her words make me feel loved. Though many at school—especially Castiel—made me feel like I am less because of my mixed blood, I never went a day thinking my mother hated me for who I am, or that I ever needed to change.

It's a pity he grew up with such hate. His family gave him so little chance to grow into anyone other than who he became.

AS THE DAY PASSES, I can ride for longer without help as my muscles remember the motions and adapt, though he eases the ache from my body whenever I need it. He teases me a few times, but the venom of the old days is always missing from his words. I can't tell whether I've grown used to it and am simply no longer bothered or if perhaps losing his family also meant losing the pressure that made him vindictive and cruel.

I try not to dwell too much on his character, reminding myself there is no need to grow close or attached to him in order for us to succeed.

By the time we arrive at the ruins of the Lunar Court, the sun has nearly set and a chill permeates the air. I dismount gingerly.

"I know you probably don't understand me, and I know you don't have a name, but I just wanted to say thank you. I've been calling you Oak in my mind, and I hope that it's okay with you," I whisper to the enormous wolf as I pet her shoulders.

She might not be from the Other Realm, but she's definitely not a typical wolf as Castiel mentioned. Perhaps she's part of a species with which the fae neglected to concern themselves with. Except for a small number—my mother included—few fae care for creatures that don't directly threaten their existence or the current state of Asteria.

We're quite the self-involved bunch.

I step away as Rowan dips his snout to receive a kiss from Castiel. The fluid familiarity of their motion makes me think they have done this a thousand times. I turn my gaze, feeling as though I'd just spied a private moment.

The golden hour washes everything in warm orange and red.

It almost makes the Lunar wasteland look welcoming.

Almost.

I untie my hair and run my fingers through the silver strands. There's a tingling on my scalp that I know is not from the tension of a full day's worth of riding.

It's from seeing the remains of the Lunar Court.

When the Dark fae ravaged the Lunar Court centuries ago, they didn't bother to clean up the lands and repurpose it, as many expected. Instead, they left the land to wither and die without its connection to Asteria's wild magic.

They didn't bother to pay respects to the bodies and bury them so they could return to nature.

They didn't even bother to protect the court with wards to prevent trespassers. But I suppose it wouldn't matter—who in their right minds would come to this broken land? What could they gain?

The answer is *nothing*.

There is nothing to gain unless you're two faeries trying to Challenge a coup.

Castiel joins me, and we stand at what looks to have been, at one point, the entrance to the court. It's hard to tell because the walls have crumbled and fallen without magic to support it.

Nature has grown wild without civilization here to hold it back. Overgrown vines and ivy climb and cover fallen stones.

Flowers I've never seen sprawl all over, making me feel like we've landed in a meadow of silver and white clashing with orange and gold.

It feels as though I've stepped into a completely different world.

Courts shouldn't look like this. Courts should be organized and clean and filled with *life*.

Chills dance along my spine as I realize my mind fills in the spaces between the ruins. My mind's eye imagines ghostly outlines of guards standing where I presume the gate is. They are faceless, but I have seen images of Lunar clothing, so their bodies are covered with swaths of silver fabric broken by midnight blue and silver-white stars. Their belts are buckled with crescent moons.

I blink, and it's gone. Only the ruins remain.

We step through the gates and my heart squeezes at the sight. I can see the beauty that lies beneath this wreckage. Though themes vary from court to court, faerie styles don't change much, so each crumbling building looks like it could be from any of our courts today.

If it weren't for the overgrown foliage, one might've thought that the devastation was wrought yesterday. There is no doubt that this is how Day will look soon if we do not succeed.

I'm still absorbed by the destruction when Castiel stands a little too close, breaking me out of my reverie. Heat rolls off his body as the remaining streaks of sunlight fade.

"Have you ever been here?" I ask.

"A few times."

I look at him, and he sighs. "As a pup, Rowan liked to explore. I fetched him from these parts more than I care to admit."

"And you never ran into any Dark faeries?"

He shakes his head. "We were lucky."

The Dark Court doesn't operate in the same way that the other courts do; since King Eldritch exiled them to their own piece of land, they could not settle on a monarch. As such, their own land withered and died without its connection to Asteria. Roaming free, sometimes Dark faeries would get together and try to ambush other courts, jealous of others' prosperity. Except for the Lunar Court, and now the Day Court, no other attempts had ever succeeded. Many theories float around about why the great Lunar fae were so easily defeated, but no one truly knows what happened. Everyone who knew the story died with the court.

Allowed to do as they wish, the Dark Court has no laws, and is ruled only by chaos.

So, it is quite the feat for Euphelia and Ryken to have successfully united and led enough Dark faeries to murder the entire Ares family. They are undeniably some of the strongest and most capable faeries of the Dark Court.

I wonder if they were the ones who brought about this destruction to the Lunar Court as well.

"Alright," Castiel leans back on his heels. "Where do we go now?"

"What do you mean?"

"Don't you know where to go?"

I stare at him, bewildered. "How would I know? You're the one who's been here before."

"Didn't the Vorukael say you'd know where to go?" He raises his eyebrows at me expectantly.

"I thought it meant there would be signs or something."

"Signs in these dead fields?"

I roll my eyes. "I don't know. Magic works in mysterious ways. Let's head to the castle first. There's bound to be some clues there."

Like our courts, the Lunar Court's castle is near the entrance, situated in the middle of what used to be a town.

I try not to look too closely at nature reclaiming what used to be the homes and lives of other fae. If I do, I might wonder, *what if this were to happen to the Night Court? What would happen to my family?*

Seeing the downfall of the Ares family, and now walking amongst the decay of the Lunar Court, has worry worming its way into my heart. We need to do something to prevent this from happening to anyone else.

My mother will not want help from any other courts, nor are they likely to extend it—even in the event of a Dark fae attack. She doesn't believe we would need help, but I feel inclined to think otherwise as we stroll past house after house of broken histories and lost memories.

We still don't know why the Dark faeries took the Day Court, and that worries me. Without knowing their motive, I cannot predict whether they're likely to come after us—or anyone else.

And while my mother is confident in our defenses, these ruins make my stomach twist uncomfortably. The Lunar Court was lauded; they were powerful in strategy and magic, and yet they fell.

I have no desire to be next.

I have to make sure Castiel survives long enough to make me his Enforcer; with my position in the Day Court, perhaps I could convince my mother to align ourselves with the Day. Standing together is better than alone.

But those are problems for another time.

We approach the debris of what used to be the Lunar Castle. Its former glory is obvious; giant, crescent moons lay cracked and broken, indicating where doors once used to stand. Thick stone pillars with engravings now filled in by moss and overgrowth lay on the ground, untouched since the day they fell.

Most of the cloth—tapestries, flags, curtains—have all disintegrated with time, devoid of the magic that sustained them.

"Devastating," Castiel mumbles as he crouches to inspect something out of my view.

"We can't let this happen to our courts," I whisper.

It is cold and overgrown with nature. Parts of the walls crumble, exposing the castle to the elements. Gaping holes where the windows used to be. Slashed portraits of old rulers still hang on the walls that remain standing. Occasionally, the tattered remains of a flag flutters, hanging on by wooden splinters. One strong gust of wind away from completely disintegrating with age.

This place must have been so full of life.

How could anyone do this?

Why would anyone do this?

I struggle to comprehend the pure malevolence of anyone who would wreak such havoc, but the image of Euphelia and Ryken springs to mind.

Wrapped in black silk and violet eyes with that red lipstick the color of fresh blood. The glee that sparkled on their countenance at the thought of violence. The black whorls and patterns marring their otherwise perfect skin.

They would do this.

Without a doubt, they were the type of faeries to revel in chaos and unrestricted power.

It is the nature of Dark fae, and it is most evident in the siblings.

I don't know whether the proclivity for violence is bred in them or whether it is simply part of their culture after fighting so long for survival. I want to believe they can be better, but it doesn't matter. It's not something we can fix—not right now, anyway.

We head straight for the throne room first—they're usually at the center of castles.

From there, we make our way throughout the halls, looking for any clues that might lead us to everfyre.

Everfyre is a magical element specific to the Lunar regions; the original flame is ever burning and never goes out. Because of its special properties, faeries of all regions used it for a plethora of reasons. While it was never common outside of the Lunar Court, it became even scarcer along with the court's downfall.

The most popular way to use pieces of everfyre was to weaponize them, such as coating weapons with the ever burning flames. While the fire would die after being used, it would take a long time before it would flicker out if left alone.

Neither of us has ever seen everfyre, but everyone has heard about it. Legend says the original flame still burns bright in its cave because only Lunar fae can access it—even those without Lunar blood can only handle everfyre for so long before the user is burned.

We spend the rest of the night exploring the castle until my sight turns bleary and my limbs feel heavy.

"We have to stop for the night," I yawn as Castiel meets me at our designated spot. "Unless you've found something."

He shakes his head, and I note with amusement that dust floats from his hair, as if even the dust can't wait to get away from the wicked prince.

"We'll have to continue tomorrow," he says. The way he looks at me makes me think there must be dust trying to escape from me, as well.

"I noticed a room with all the walls still up. Only one bed, but I'm sure it won't be a problem." His smirk has me blushing to the tips of my ears, and I'm both a little disgusted with myself and glad for the darkness hiding it.

I'd heard him say such things with many a faerie before—especially while we were in the Academy—but never directed at me. I suppose when he's fighting for his life and stuck with only one other faerie, even I can seem good enough to flirt with.

"No, it won't be a problem. You can have the floor." I tilt my head and dare him to refuse me.

He only shakes his head, but a chuckle fills the halls as he turns.

CHAPTER NINE

I WAKE UP ON THE FLOOR.

As tired as I was, I should have been more suspicious when Castiel graciously let me take the bed. The cloud of dust that sprang forth when I sat on it was enough to choke every faerie in the vicinity. No amount of magic was going to clean that thoroughly enough for me to lie in it.

He laughed until I sent shadows crawling up his ankles to shackle his legs together.

Then it was my turn to laugh.

In the end, we took our own corners on the room's floor.

As I blink away the sleep, sky-blue eyes stare down at me, a smirk of amusement making its way across his face.

"You are not pretty in the morning."

I glare at him and scramble to get up.

"How are you awake so early?" The sun is barely over the mountains; the world is just waking up.

"Day faerie," he shrugs.

"How long have you been up?" I grumble, annoyed that he hadn't woken me with him.

"Long enough. There's a river near here, by the way. You really need it."

I rub my eyes and glare at him, only to realize his messy hair is drenched.

THE COLD WATER SHOCKS my mind and body awake. It's refreshing and different from the showers and baths I've had of late—washing in a river reminds me of simpler times when Elysia, Alfynia, and I were younger.

I always knew I was destined for my mother's throne—as long as no one wrenched it from her cold, dead hands—but it never felt real to me.

Even now, it feels strange to have accepted this quest and be doing all of this just so I could avoid accepting queenship. Other faeries might say I am ungrateful or rash. Or even a spoiled brat.

After all, I am a halfling, and many pure-blooded high faeries would trade an arm to be in my position.

But I know, deep in my heart, I am not meant to be queen of the Night Court. It's not who I am.

I grew up with them. I wear their colors. I know their history and I would give my life for them any day.

But I am not made to be their Queen.

Maybe it is my human side, but the power of the monarchy doesn't entice me. I am better when I am in the shadows. Better when I am unnoticed. Being the monarch's Enforcer is much more fitting for me.

And that's why I need Castiel to survive. I need to win this so he can reclaim his throne and I can take my rightful place as an Enforcer, rather than a Queen.

I bite back the small thought that whispers: *am I convincing myself, or reassuring myself I'm better in the shadows?*

When I return feeling a little cleaner, Castiel hands me a small, roasted bird on a stick.

"Eat," he says without an explanation.

"Where did you get this? Did you steal it from the Dark Court?" My eyes grow wide. Magic has limitations. The farther an item is, the harder it is to call forth. We can create certain things from thin air, but they are usually weaker or hold no substance. Things cleaned by magic are not as clean as they can be. Magically created food would not fill us. If he conjured this bird, it would have had to come from somewhere. The closest place is the Dark Court.

"What? No. I can take it back if you don't want it." He reaches forward, but I snatch my hand back.

"I never said that. I Just wanted to know where it was from."

"Take it or leave it."

I take a bite and it... is surprisingly good. "Why are you secretive about this?"

"I caught it, okay?"

I nearly choke on a piece of the meat.

"You did?"

"Yes," he sighs. "If I'd have known you'd have so many stupid questions about me, I'd have come without you. Better to face the serpent alone and die than to endure this insufferable interrogation."

"Wait, wait, wait," I laugh. "I didn't say this was *bad*."

"Your face said it all."

"No, that's not what I meant." I mask my amusement and sober up. "I'm just shocked you're a half decent hunter, that's all."

His eyes narrow. "Why wouldn't I be?"

"Were you even at the Academy?" I finish the last bite and wipe my mouth, feeling a lot better now that I'm clean and full. "You showed absolutely no interest in anything at school. You put in zero effort to any training. I'm just shocked you didn't show your true self there. That's all."

He ignores me and grumbles something I can't hear, turning around to stomp back to the castle.

I do my best to hold in a giggle. Alone like this, he seems to be a completely different person than the bully I knew at the Academy. It does not erase any of the cruel things he's done in the past, nor does it excuse him, but it helps me to understand him better as a person.

And, strangely enough, I'm finding that I don't hate this side of him as much as I thought I would.

Depending on how this goes, we might even be able to co-exist in peace one day.

IT'S WELL INTO THE night and I'm exhausted. We've been searching the castle all day, going through each room and hall with a fine-toothed comb without knowing quite what we are searching for, hoping we would know it by instinct. We should have saved time without a wash this morning, because I am definitely dirtier now than I was before we started this.

"Library!" Castiel's voice echoes loudly enough throughout the halls to unsettle the dust.

I make my way down the hall, trying not to choke on the dust or trip over debris.

"You think that the books that *may* have survived the attack will lead us there?" Fed up with the air, I wave a hand and clear the air for a few seconds of reprieve.

He stands by the remnants of a wall and a heavy gust of wind blows through. There goes the dust again. "No. But I think we can see where it might be."

"It will not be that obvious." I give him a little push and stand by the giant hole in the wall that might have once been a window. He exudes warmth, but I leave extra space between us despite the chilling wind.

The castle lives atop a cliff, and the library sits at its highest part. The view takes my breath away.

The moon, a little fuller than it was days ago, is now high in the sky. It illuminates everything with a silvery glow. The ruins below us look less devastating and more... like art and history.

Hauntingly beautiful.

Castiel points. I squint and notice a clearing in the distance that feels like it's where we need to go. Everfyre was precious to the Lunar Court, but it was difficult to obtain; simply knowing where to find it didn't mean that every Lunar faerie could get some. I only hope there's enough magic in the everfyre's protection wards to keep it intact, but not so much that I won't be able to get a piece.

"Are you talking about that glow? I can barely see it, but I think you're right. It seems like more than just moonlight."

"What are you talking about?" His eyes turn to me and for the first time, I notice they have a slight reflection to them—sort of like a cat's. Or maybe it's a golden hue.

"That spot there," I point.

"You mean the little clearing that looks different from the others?"

"Yes, but there's a little light radiating from it. See, it just pulsed. Definitely not moonlight."

He turns to me again and his brows furrow.

"Flower, there's no light."

My heart beats a little faster, but frustration blooms in my chest and overshadows any confusing feelings that might arise before I can study them. "This is not the time to be messing around."

Something in his eyes makes me look again.

"But it's... it's there," I say lamely.

He shakes his head as realization dawns on his face. "Maybe this is what the Vorukael was talking about. It must be there."

"If we hurry, we can get there before the sun comes up," I say, turning to leave the library.

"Hold on."

I turn, and he has his fingers in his mouth. A loud whistle pierces the air, and a black rift tears into the space between us.

Rowan comes bounding through the darkness, landing softer than I expect for an animal of his size. His tail thumps against the floor, sending waves of dust and debris into the air.

I squeeze my eyes shut and cough, yelling at him to stop.

When I open my eyes, I look into his apologetic gaze and instantly feel guilty. I apologize, and he lets his tongue hang out.

"Hey," Castiel crosses over to his wolf in two long strides and wraps his arms around Rowan's neck. "How are you?"

"Good to see you, Rowan," I grin at the giant canine. "Shouldn't you have called him from outside, though? That tail is going to do some damage around here." I wave my arms around the floating dust in vain. Even my magic can't fend it off for long.

"We're taking a shortcut." Castiel pats Rowan's back and nods. With a quick heave, he throws himself over the wolf and settles in without a saddle.

"I guess I'll meet you downstairs?" I mean to make a statement, but it ends up sounding like a question.

He nods at me, indicating for me to copy him.

Something twists uncomfortably in my chest at the thought of jumping onto Rowan's back behind Castiel, but I brush it off.

"We're going through there?" I point at the giant gaping hole in the wall.

He nods.

I point again and make sure to do so more fervently just to confirm we're on the same page.

He rolls his eyes. "Rowan's from the Other Realm, remember? Get on. We're losing moonlight here."

Neither of us have powers of flight, so if we fall, we could die.

But he's adamant.

I clench my teeth and grab a fistful of black fur. With a heave, I jump onto Rowan's back.

Castiel stiffens as I settle in, but I am just as stiff. My arms feel clumsy as I wrap them around his middle and try not to focus on how solid he feels for someone who is so awful at any sort of combat.

But then I remember his enormous bow. It might have been lighter than expected, but drawing and aiming it was no easy feat.

What more does this princeling hide?

I grab my forearms to avoid touching him more than necessary, but to my horror, it's hard not to lean into his warmth.

Before I can tell them to wait, the giant wolf takes two steps back and lunges forward. I feel Rowan's muscles flex, and fear grabs at my throat as he jumps.

Suddenly, we're in the air.

The castle is behind us, and the ground is so far away.

So far down.

I dare not look. Panic clamps around my chest, tightening my lungs.

My fingers claw at Castiel's shirt, fisting the cloth and holding on for life. I pull him to me and hang on with everything I have.

Warmth wraps around the back of my hand and envelops it completely, drawing me back to my senses.

My heart pounds so hard that I don't register it at first, but then I realize he's placed his hand on mine. The heat from his hand somehow calms my panic from a raging storm to a quiet thud.

I open my eyes.

We fall toward the land that continues to take my breath away.

Despite the icy wind that whips around my face bringing tears to my eyes, it feels as though Rowan is *gliding* through the air. The reach of his leap is so far that he doesn't seem afraid at all; it's as if he's simply jumping from one log to another.

Except this is far deadlier.

We're still plummeting toward the ground, but gold sparkles surround us, preventing the harshest of the windchills.

Before I can fully appreciate the surrounding sights, the ground rushes toward us all too quickly. I want to shut my eyes, but I don't. I tighten my core and brace for landing.

I watch as the ground approaches. I feel as Rowan lands gracefully.

I don't have time to speak before his muscles flex again under my legs and he runs at full speed.

The wind whips against my face and without thinking, I tuck myself behind Castiel's back, taking solace in his heat. It feels comforting. It feels safe.

It takes a while to adjust, but when I finally relax, he speaks.

I try to ignore the rumble of his chest under my arms, but I notice that he's taken his hand off mine. I don't know when that happened, but I'm glad for it.

"Rowan's a lot faster than his wolf friends." He explains tightly, as though he feels the need to justify our proximity.

A rush of relief floods through me. As much as I try to ignore the details of what he told the Vorukael to get us here, I admit it sometimes haunts the corners of my mind—especially when he's revealed so much of his true self that I can barely recognize him anymore.

I don't know what to make of his confession—if I can even call it as such—but I know that while I may hate him marginally less, my feelings for him have transformed only from pure hatred to begrudging partnership. I refuse to let it be any more.

A TWIST OF NIGHT AND DAY

Without a doubt, I know once we are no longer isolated with just each other for company, a working partnership will be all that's left of this journey.

I'm more than fine with that.

Rowan is as graceful as he is quick. Though the forest here is both dark and dense, he hasn't stumbled even once.

His steps are well-timed, well-aimed, and he seems to know exactly where he's headed before his paws have left the ground.

Though I have little experience with wolves, I can sense his intelligence and his superiority. How many more wolves like Rowan run around in the Other Realm? What other creatures reside there?

I would hate to be on the receiving end of his ferocity.

The forest grows sparser and sparser until we arrive at a small clearing. In the middle of it, as if put on a spotlight by the moon, is a large boulder with an opening like a cave. It is at least the height of three faeries; the boulder looks both fae-made and natural at the same time. The moonlight washes the rock in mystical hues of white, grey, and shadows. The mouth is pitch black. In my heart, I know it leads into a tunnel deep in Asteria where all fae should be afraid.

The magic here is strong even centuries after the decimation of the Lunar fae. The boulder itself emanates power, and though it feels like the magic is trapped behind a veil, I can still feel it rolling off the cave's mouth in waves.

I slide off Rowan's back before Castiel does, landing lightly on my feet despite the long ride; my riding muscles have since woken.

The area is clear of forest debris except for some displaced leaves and twigs likely kicked up by animals. The overgrown grass has a strange glow—not strong enough to be blinding, but definitely unmistakable. It's not as though the grass reflects the moon, but rather like it absorbs the moonlight and then emanates the glow from each blade.

No marks on the ground indicate any protective charms. No visible walls surround the area. But neither do I hear the forest nightlife.

It is as if nature itself can feel the thick magic that sizzles in the air, warning life to stay away.

When I take a step closer, something thrums in my veins like it's answering a question that the cave poses.

It wants me to enter.

I hesitate. Every faerie knows that when something calls to us, we need to be wary. Just like with the lost fae who call and tempt us when we realmwalk, there are older beings who could pose as a significant danger to faeries.

"What are you waiting for?" Castiel approaches the cave's mouth, but Rowan shakes his head and chuffs.

"Wait—don't you feel it?"

"Feel what?" He looks back and forth between me and the shaggy wolf, confused. "What is it?" He asks Rowan.

"That," I wave my hands in the air. "The magic. The call."

He gives me a weird look.

"The *urging*," I press.

Suddenly, realization dawns. "You don't feel it, do you?"

He shrugs. "I guess that's what the Vorukael meant, right? *You'll know?*"

Rowan glances at me nervously as Castiel strides confidently toward the cave's mouth.

"I'll be fine," he nods to the wolf.

I silently open my hands and call my sword, letting the midnight sparkles spread forth from the middle of my palm outwards. My sword blinks into existence and I close my fingers around the hilt, taking comfort in its familiar weight.

My sword is one of my most prized possessions. It is made of old fae magic and specially tailored to me. It sings in my hands as I sheath it, asking me for blood.

I follow him toward the mouth, anxiety dampened only slightly by my sword hanging heavy and familiar at my hip.

Suddenly, Rowan lets out a long whine. My head snaps at a loud sizzling sound.

Castiel lands heavily on his back, his eyes wide with shock.

"What—how—" He sputters, looking from me to Rowan.

Rowan dips his head and snorts.

They have a conversation I don't pay attention to; I pull my sword out of its sheath and hold it at my side as I walk toward the cave, every muscle tense.

"Wait—" He reaches out but freezes as I step into the cave.

His navy eyes fill with confusion. He stands up and makes his way toward me, only for Rowan to whine again.

He reaches forward and immediately rips his hand back, wincing and whipping it in the air to cool it.

"I guess I can't go in..." he whispers, staring at the spot where the invisible shield crackled to life and sizzled against his skin.

I take a deep breath. "I guess not."

I'm relieved. Castiel might be a decent healer, but he's not a fighter. If there's anything down there that I'll have to fight, it will be best if he stays up here.

Though... Dark faeries roam these lands.

"Stay with Rowan. Or better yet, find a hiding spot with Rowan and try not to die, okay?"

He sends me a glare but acquiesces. He has no other choice.

Gulping, I adjust my grip on the hilt and take a step forward.

CHAPTER TEN

I CLENCH MY JAW SHUT and steel myself to take another step. A small ball of grey-blue fire blinks into existence when I snap my fingers, shining enough light so I can see the plain dirt walls that surround me.

There are no lanterns or any support beams to keep the tunnel from collapsing, but it stays structurally sound, held up by magic of the land.

I hope.

As I suspected, the tunnel goes further underground than I can see with the light of faefyre at my side. Faefyre is utterly harmless, but it projects enough light that I feel a little safer being able to see.

My fyre has always been a little different from other Night faeries' because I'm half-human. Others, like Castiel and his friends, made fun of me because it's a shade lighter than typical, but I'm just glad I can make faefyre at all. After years of struggling, I can finally make it blink into existence at my will.

Right now, its lighter color is more useful than the traditional Night faeries' Dark faefyre, anyway. In this ominous tunnel, it seems even brighter than usual.

The tunnel I travel into is not steep, but it's long and it's finally opened enough so I have space to spread my arms freely.

Which means there's enough space to swing my sword properly in case I need to.

I don't know how long I walk, surrounded by nothing but dirt and darkness, but after the initial flat entranceway, the slope downward increases dramatically.

The tunnel feels like old magic—dangerous and ancient in ways I think even my mother would not have recognized. With the fae's tendency for apathy, archaic magic and methods are often lost over time.

And yet, my body seems to know this place. The cave is a question my magic wants to answer.

Despite the fear I keep pushing to the back of my mind, despite the apprehension I feel the deeper I go, something within me stirs.

I don't understand it, but I know that answers might be at the end of the tunnel.

And perhaps that scares me more than I care to admit.

A chill has set into my bones by the time a faraway glow indicates I've finally reached the end.

My faefyre will follow wherever I go, so I don't have to worry about light. Instead, I draw a few more daggers from my reserve and tuck them in various places beneath my clothes—just in case.

I steady myself and grab the handle of my sword with both hands, trying to ignore the loud pounding in my ears so I can focus on my breathing and prepare for... for what? I don't know. I've never heard much about everfyre except for its usage in battle. No one talked about how to get it or what I would need to do in order to get a piece.

Adrenaline courses through my body as I get closer to the bottom.

My entire body is alive, buzzing with energy. Nothing else matters when I'm like this—only the mission is important.

Sticking to the wall, I inch forward until I can see past the opening into the enormous, rounded room with walls carved from dark stone.

It's taller than I can make out without craning my head, but what captures my attention is the blue flame that sits atop a raised platform in the middle.

I know what it is the moment I lay eyes on it.

The everfyre is enormous, taking up almost a third of the space as it flickers with life; though bits of orange and red occasionally peek through, it is mostly blue and deep purples highlighted by flames of silver and white.

The air is charged with the electric magic of the everfyre. Its tips curl and lick at the air, hungry and alive. It's unlike any other magic I've ever felt before. It calls to me, a quiet and subtle urging.

I tear my eyes from the mesmerizing flame and am sorry to do so, but I need to survey the room.

The cave's walls appear to be carved of the same dark rock as the ground. The everfyre's glow is the only source of light in the room except for a small opening at the very top—so small I can barely make it out and much too far to reach—but a small stream of light leaks through until it reaches the everfyre and becomes engulfed within its brightness. Wordlessly, I silence my faefyre. I won't be needing it with the everfyre here.

There doesn't seem to be a guard of any sort, but just because no beast stands around doesn't mean there isn't anyone waiting. There are also no visible marks on the ground to show any active wards, but I still wish I had a stone to throw so I can test the theory.

Tentatively, I take a step forward, keeping my muscles coiled and my hand tight on my sword.

I get five steps in when a silvery glow appears in the air.

My heart pounds as I slow to a stop and wait.

The light is similar in shape to the dark rift that opens during realmwalking. My breath hitches.

A faerie steps out from the light.

"Hello," I greet her and hope my voice doesn't betray the thunderous pounding of my heart. I fight the urge to wipe my hands on my pants, tightening my grip on my sword instead.

She smiles; her hair is silver, like mine, but it's so long it pools at her feet. She wears robes that are ancient even to our faerie styles. No jewels drip from her earlobes, and the tips of her ears are uncapped, showing they're not as pointed as the ears of today's faeries. Her neck and wrists are bare of chains or any other decoration.

I shiver when I look into her eyes.

They are pure white.

"I'm Astrid Vanaguard of the Night Court. Who are you?" I keep my voice strong and stable like I'm not quaking in my boots.

She tilts her head, and I think she looks at me with amusement, but I'm not sure.

"My name is Freyin, and it's been a long time since I've seen one like you." Her voice is odd; it's like the sound of running my hands along a scroll, but like the Vorukael's, I can't tell if she is speaking in my head or out loud.

A TWIST OF NIGHT AND DAY

A part of me feels crushed; even this strange faerie can tell I'm a halfling.

But no matter. I'm here for a job, and I will get it done.

"I assume you know why I'm here?" I mean to make a statement, but it comes out sounding like a question instead. I don't know why, but the tips of my ears warm at the mistake.

"You're here for a piece of everfyre." She tilts her head.

"Are you here to stop me?" I blurt. My heart races and I can feel magic pooling in my hands, itching for release. My sword almost quivers with eagerness for action.

"I do not stop anyone from getting pieces of everfyre—I simply make sure they are worthy of it by posing a challenge."

Another challenge. Great.

"What is it? I'll do it."

"You simply have to best me in battle." She opens her arms as though welcoming me to her realm.

I answer after a long pause. "Why is it difficult to defeat you?"

"Who says it is difficult?"

"You wouldn't be here if it weren't."

"Ah," she closes her arms. "I'm an Elder assigned to the everfyre as its protector, but it is not my prisoner. I do not stop those who are worthy of taking a piece—I only make sure those who retrieve their pieces are worthy of it. Many have defeated me before and taken their pieces home to share with their warriors."

I narrow my eyes, doing my best to suppress the chill that wracks through my body. Another Elder One? How am I to defeat an Elder?

"What sort of challenge is it?"

"Combat," she says, crossing her arms. "I am able to discern many things about a faerie based only on one battle, and a fight to the death is not one in which many are willing to participate."

My heart races. My mouth is a desert and swallowing doesn't help. *Fighting* an Elder? Summoning and trapping the Vorukael was a different matter—in fact, now that I think about it, the Vorukael probably allowed himself to be caught, given how easily he left my iron and ash circle.

Can I win?

"I will fight you," I croak.

She smiles so brightly that for a split moment, I am afraid I've made a mistake. But there is no choice. I force my breathing to even. I feel the tang of magic rest on my tongue.

I am here, and I will do this.

And I will win.

My mind empties except for the thrill of the battle. I recall the lessons that I learned; the endless hours of morning and night time practice. I remember the sparring I did with my sisters.

Freyin does not change her clothes, but thin, twin blades appear in her hands. She crosses them in front of her chest, running them along each other. The sound of metal on metal makes my skin crawl.

I look her in the eyes and know she is ready.

But am I?

No way out now.

I drop into a fighting stance as my vision sharpens to focus on Freyin. My sword is balanced in such a way that I can use it with one hand or both, but I choose to begin with one so my other hand is free for magic. I have a feeling I'll need it to learn how she moves.

In the blink of an eye, she's crossed the distance between us, and I'm blocking her blade. For someone with such a small frame, she's incredibly strong. As it always is with the fae, looks are deceiving.

Magic flickers at the tips of my fingers when she suddenly retreats.

I almost stumble from the loss of pressure.

She comes at me again with both swords, and I duck.

I sweep my leg. She jumps in time, pointing both swords down at me as she drops. I push my hand into the air and sparks of midnight magic jump from my palm.

She rolls mid-air.

Freyin lands neatly on the other side of the cave, throwing her sword at me so smoothly that I almost don't see the thin blade until it's too late.

I roll, narrowly avoiding death-by-giant-needle. I don't look back when I hear the sword clang against the wall. She's already recalled the weapon.

The taste of magic barely flickers on my tongue. I dodge by instinct. A sphere of deadly silvery and white magic bursts into sparks as it makes contact with the stone wall where I stood just moments ago.

In a flash, she's on me again. Our blades make contact and I grit my teeth against the ringing, digging my heels into the ground to keep from being pushed.

We stay locked in a dance that lasts for longer than I care; all I know is my muscles are weary and my movements have slowed, while hers have not changed.

Back and forth, I fight to stall for time as I watch her patterns and read her motions. It takes longer than I'm used to; I don't like to attack before I've learned my opponents, but because I can usually read my opponents almost right away, battles don't last long.

I breathe out the frustration and refocus. This is my element. This is where I feel most like myself and most confident. This is what I know.

It takes a little more time, but as I feel myself slow, I see the twitch of her lip and know in my heart that she's about to advance.

I've learned her cues.

I attack first.

She raises both swords to block my slash.

I press harder, using both hands to push. I have the upper hand here. For a moment, I think I see a flash of fear in her eyes.

Suddenly, something jabs my side. I cry out, rolling to break my fall.

I bounce up and look around. What happened? I didn't feel the tingle of magic in the air, and both her hands were in my view—so how did she—?

Then I see it.

Her long white hair floats behind her, defiant of gravity. It's shaped like a thick whip, moving with a mind of its own. I guess it moves with undetectable magic.

Freyin grins madly.

"I forgot to tell you, didn't I?" She looks lovingly at her hair before locking eyes with me.

A TWIST OF NIGHT AND DAY

Panic bubbles, and I swallow hard to keep it down. I could scream that this isn't fair, but life isn't always fair. This is just the latest problem I have to deal with.

For the next moments, I am on the defense again. I let her lunge at me and attack me from all sides: two swords and a whip made of hair.

I keep one hand off my sword to throw up shields; I've gone from defending against one faerie with two swords to protecting myself on three fronts. As we continue, I realize her hair is more like a small serpent than a whip. It seems to have a mind of its own, attacking me from the sides while I'm busy defending against Freyin's blades.

It isn't easy, but I bide my time watching her movements and learning how her magical hair works.

Eventually, I figure out its cues, too.

But not before I'm battered, bruised, and struggling to stay upright.

In this dim underground cave, the blue glow of the everfyre gives her a mystical look that would strike terror into my very soul if I only paused to think about it.

So, I do not pause, focusing only on the battle and how to win.

I continue to block and parry, planning my next few steps before I make them.

I settle on trying to cut her hair off.

She comes for me, but I am ready and dodge at the last moment. Every time we have done this move, I jumped back.

Not this time.

This time, I twirl and slam my elbow into her spine. She crumples, caught by surprise.

As she falls, I wrap my hand with the ends of her hair and yank with every ounce of strength I could muster, slashing my sword down at the same time.

A growl of frustration rips through me when my sword doesn't cut through, but I'm not surprised.

I wrench her hair again and let go at the last moment. She loses balance before jumping backward in retreat; the serpent-hair is not happy with me.

She laughs, and her wind chime laugh surrounds me, reminding me of the Vorukael.

The Vorukael.

He told me the everfyre would get me to the everfyre. At the time, I didn't know what he meant.

As Freyin pushes herself up from the floor, the everfyre's blue glow flickers against her pale skin and hair. An idea forms, and I think I finally understand.

I charge, but she recovers in time—as I expected.

She needles at me with her thin swords as a distraction while her hair floats up into the air to strike.

I see it in my periphery and dodge in such a way that I grab a fistful of the writhing hair in midair.

She expects me to elbow her, so I bring a knee up.

Before she can recover, I kick her in the stomach with all my force.

She soars. I get a running start—except I run away from her, instead of toward her.

I race to the evrefyre, pumping magic into my legs in preparation so I can run faster and jump higher.

At the last second, I launch myself into the air and sail across the tops of the flames that reach out for me as if in a greeting, licking at my feet.

I drag my sword through the blue flames and hope that it works. I hope I have not misinterpreted the Vorukael.

The thud of my feet landing on the rocky ground echos in the chamber. The pounding in my ears is broken only by the crackling of blue flames coating my sword from the hilt to the very tip.

I don't have time to admire it.

I swivel to face Freyin, whose eyes are glowing not with malice or disapproval, but with... amusement?

We clash again, the sound of metal on metal screeching in my ears.

But this time, I notice she's not attacking with the same ferocity. She's not holding back, but she's more apprehensive. More wary of my sword that's now wrapped in blue flames.

I use it to my advantage.

Now that I recognize her cues and can almost predict what her next step is, stopping her in her tracks is easier—especially since she's more careful.

She shifts her weight onto one foot.

I charge.

Thrusting my sword forward, we dance back and forth until I find an opening. She spreads her fingers and I taste the tang of magic.

I twist, pulling her arm forward and under mine, then knee her square in the chest in one motion. She stumbles and falls on her back.

She tries to turn, but I'm already straddling her. My left hand is open and holding a shield to protect myself from her swords and her magical hair. My right keeps my sword close enough that the sharp point barely skims her throat. It is so close that the blue flames lick her skin.

"Well done," she smiles, dropping her own swords which fall with a hollow clang. "Are you not going to kill me now? You should do it quickly, lest I think of a way out of this predicament."

I shake my head and lower my sword. My adrenaline is still going and my eyes track her movements in case I was wrong as I unfold myself, letting my shield disappear and offering her my hand.

She takes it, and I help her stand.

"I don't need to kill you; you said I only had to best you." I pant as I speak.

She gives me a look of intrigue, and I continue.

"You *implied* I needed to kill you in order to win, but you didn't *say* I needed to kill you. You only explicitly said that I was to defeat you." I pause. "And now I have. Can I have a piece of the everfyre?"

She nods thoughtfully. "Only certain people recognize this. Those who don't rarely succeed."

Electricity zings in my body as I try to calm down from the adrenaline.

What if I made a mistake? What if she meant for me to kill her after all? I mentally shake my head. That wouldn't make sense.

She looks at me with those thoughtful white eyes. I'm afraid to look into them, because I think I see the world in those eyes. I realize she has more power than she showed. She probably has more power than I can imagine.

Finally, she smiles and I feel as though I am free to breathe again.

She opens her hand, palms facing up, and I can't help but flinch. She is kind enough to not mention it.

White magic blossoms in her palms, and a small glass jar appears.

"This will hold one flame. It will burn so long as you keep it in this jar. Once it is removed, you can light your weapons as you did with your sword. It will not re-ignite once extinguished."

I wet my lips and tear my eyes away from her to look at my flickering sword. "What will extinguish it?"

"You can put out the flame with your mind once you've achieved your task. If you do not put it out, the flame will slowly diminish over time until it is gone."

"And if I need more?"

"I have deemed you as worthy. You may collect more flames as needed in the future," she nods. Thankfully, I've run out of questions because she disappears just as she appeared, walking into a white rift in the air.

I'm left alone in the empty chamber, holding my sword and the glass jar that's only about the size of an apple. I take a few laps around the chamber to see if there are any hints on how to transfer a flame into the jar, but am dismayed to find none. There is only black rock surrounding me.

Finally, I decide to use my sword. It worked once before—it should work again, right?

I walk up to the roaring blue everfyre and tentatively dip my sword in, cringing as the flames lick the ancient steel, merging with the fire that already coats it.

Now that I'm not in the middle of fighting for my life, I worry the flames may damage my sword—but it doesn't appear to be an issue. Heat from the flames warms my hand all the way to my forearm, but it doesn't burn me.

I count to ten before gingerly pulling it out. Carefully, I aim the tip of my sword at the entrance of the jar and watch, mesmerized, as a tiny blue fire jumps into the jar. Turning my favorite blade, I note with pleasure that the size of the flames on it has not diminished at all.

A tiny fire floats in the jar, alive and writhing with ancient magic.

All energy disappears from my body as I turn to leave.

I stumble and fall. Horror fills my body as the jar flies out of my hands and drops.

My heart stops with the crack it makes as it crashes onto the floor.

But it doesn't break. The flame flickers happily as if nothing happened.

I sigh with relief and let myself lay on the cold ground for a moment. My limbs are sacks of rocks. Trying to think is like trying to see through the thickest winter fog. I have no energy and no magic left. Only a tired fire runs in my veins, and the floor of this cave is the only thing tempering the heat.

I didn't realize the fight with Freyin left me so depleted—I could not call forth a single faefyre even if I tried. The *thought* of trying makes me close my eyes. As the cool floor chases from my body the last drop of adrenaline, I am left with aches and pains all over.

It's an odd feeling; I'm not used to feeling so drained after a battle. More often than not, I leave a battle more invigorated than when I began it.

A few long breaths later, I gather enough courage to push myself up.

Biting back a groan, I finally have both my sword and the everfyre in my hands, though I nearly topple when picking them up. I close my eyes and focus—it's so hard to form even a string of coherent thought, much less command magic. It takes three tries, but a small ball of fire finally sputters to life. It's more silver and midnight blue now, but I'm too tired to care. All I care about is that it moves in sync with my footsteps, staying several steps ahead of me as I drag myself toward the tunnels.

The battle with Freyin left me broken and exhausted, and the pain only intensifies with each heavy step.

I limp into the darkness, lit only by the faefyre. I've had rough fights before, but I've never felt this tired. It's like my insides have been scrambled and put back together only to be tossed around again. It's like my entire mind and soul have shrunken and shrivelled into one little raisin.

I don't know how long I limp for, but when I finally see the sky from the mouth of the cave, I almost cry with relief.

I'm not far from the opening when my vision starts to fade. Something prickles under my skin and I realize with horror that Freyin must have used some form of poison that escaped my notice. Maybe that's why I'm *so tired*.

My knees buckle. I trip.

A blur jumps into my darkening vision and I feel a tug right before everything goes black.

CHAPTER ELEVEN

WHERE AM I?

I open my eyes to a log ceiling. I'm on a hard bed of some sort.

Every bone in my body aches. Every muscle is on fire. I groan quietly, pushing myself up to look around.

The bed I am on appears to be at one end of a small cabin that has not been occupied in a long time.

Sunlight peers in through panes of clear magic covering the windows like glass to prevent windchill. Other than the windows and the thin layer of dust and overgrowth, the cabin resembles any other small home I would expect to find in the edges of the Night Court.

I almost swing my legs over the bed when I realize Rowan is curled up on the ground, looking up at me with intelligent and questioning silver eyes.

Pressing my palms to my eyes, memories of a black blur and of being pulled fill my mind.

"Did you save me?" I ask. "Thank you for doing so."

He blinks at me and tilts his head. I hope he means *you're welcome*.

Gingerly, I step around Rowan, who watches me but doesn't move. The cabin is small and without room dividers, but it appears to be in the shape of an L.

I pad quietly around the corner, suspicious but trying to remember that Rowan would not have been calm if there was danger around.

A small fire crackles in the fireplace and on a large, clean silver dish sits a pair of roasted rabbits.

Beside the table is Castiel, stretched out and sleeping on a couch, legs dangling off the armrest. I pad into the room and scoff to myself.

Any half-decent warrior with a sense of self-preservation would have woken up as soon as I stepped off the bed.

My body still cries in pain, but my stomach's complaints are far louder. I turn around to the bathroom I noticed earlier and get started on the basics.

There's no mirror and I don't dare try the overgrown shower, but the sink looks like it's been recently used.

Moments later, I emerge feeling a little more like myself.

With a wave of my hand, a space on the ground clears of dust. I take a seat and tear a leg from a rabbit, my mouth salivating.

The cabin is neat, but has clearly been unoccupied for some time. There is a large hole in the wall above the fireplace, but like the windows, it also has been filled in with a clear pane of magic to keep the warmth in.

As I tear into my second piece, Castiel finally stirs. I'm still not sure he notices me; he yawns and rubs his eyes before looking around.

I'm continually shocked by his lack of self-preservation instincts.

His light blue eyes widen slightly when he finally catches sight of me. Propping himself to sit, he runs a hand through his hair warily.

"Feeling better?"

"Much, thank you," I answer between mouthfuls. "Was this you?"

He nods, not taking his eyes off me.

I pause. "Do I have something on my face?"

"More like all over you."

"What?" There hadn't been a mirror in the bathroom, but I was so hungry I didn't care to check myself.

"You're..." His eyes narrow in thought. "You've been poisoned by something I can't quite discern. This is the first time you've been properly awake in two days."

Ice passes through me. *Two days?*

"How is... how is that possible?" I put the rabbit down and try to recount the last thing I remember.

Leaving the tunnel... black blur. Then, here.

Nothing in between.

He continues looking at me warily, and it makes me uneasy. Like he's waiting for something to happen.

"I think it's about to take hold again," he warns.

"What—" Suddenly, my muscles burn. My head pounds. Hot tears fill my eyes. Something is tearing me apart from the inside.

My entire body is on fire. I let out something like a whimper.

Castiel stands sharply and makes his way over. I think I reach out for him, because his hands are reaching out to me. He catches me before I hit the floor.

The room spins. The colors blend. I can't tell up from down or left from right.

Until his worried blue eyes fill my vision and anchor me.

"It's okay," he coos like he has done this before. "I've got you."

And as my eyes close, I believe him.

SOMETIMES, I WAKE UP, and Rowan's snout is in my face, sniffing me.

Sometimes, I wake up, and it's Castiel's eyes hovering over me.

I never wake up alone, though.

My memories fade in and out along with my consciousness.

Castiel wakes me up to feed me.

His hands sometimes hover over my body, and warmth emanates from them, lulling me back to sleep.

THE FIRST THING I SEE is the now familiar log ceiling. Castiel has dragged a chair over, and he sleeps in it next to the bed. Rowan sleeps silently on the ground.

The headboard shows three ticks—I assume I've been ill for three days since we got here—which means we're almost out of time. We only have two days left to complete the Challenge.

I gulp as I remember my words from the night before.

"Don't go," I whisper, clutching onto his sleeves as he props my limp body up.

In my delirious state, I had asked him to stay.

And he had.

Castiel's hair is pushed back like he's run his hand through it a million times. Dark smudges have developed under his eyes. His chest rises and falls slowly.

I don't want to wake him because he clearly needs the rest. Rowan watches silently as I tiptoe past the two of them. He raises his fluffy head when I head for the bathroom, but I put a finger to my lips and point to Castiel. Rowan's head settles back on his paws and he closes his eyes, though I can see his ears twitch in my direction.

I relieve myself and brush my teeth with a toothbrush from my reserve. The shower still looks unusable, so a cleaning charm will have to do. Remembering the way Castiel looked at me, I conjure a mirror.

A heavy ball of horror grows in my stomach as I study myself.

Faint blue lines cover one side of my face, pulsing lightly. Similar lines spread down the bare skin on my arms. Pulling my pants up reveals the same blue patterns all over.

What the—

I shake my head and make the mirror disappear with a wave of my hand. As long as I'm well enough to think and move, we have a mission to complete; I can deal with this later.

Opening the door, I step back when Castiel stands on the other side, glaring down at me.

"You could have woken me," he growls.

"You needed the sleep," I answer. I try to hide how sheepish I feel; even though he's helped me for days, I still don't feel comfortable around him.

He sighs. "How do you feel? Did you eat?"

I shake my head. "I just got up. I feel okay except for..." I wave at my face and body.

"Yeah, it's been like that for a few days," he glances at me warily. I would have warmed under his gaze, but I know he's just studying the strange blue patterns and whirls.

"On the bright side, they seem to be fading," he shakes his head.

We switch places and he takes the bathroom while I start hungrily on the roasted birds on the coffee table, feeling like I haven't eaten in days.

He's not a bad cook. He's not a bad healer. He can talk to animals, and he has a pet wolf from the Other Realm. A month ago, if anyone had tried to convince me that these were all true about Castiel, I'd have laughed in their face. Even a week ago, I'd have shaken my head.

Now, he and his wolf are feeding me and keeping me alive.

He emerges from the bathroom looking a little more alert. Somehow, his white clothes have stayed perfectly clean this entire time.

"Still doing okay?" He grunts as he brushes past me to grab a small roasted bird.

I nod, but fear wracks through me as I remember the little glass jar. Freyin said I could take more if I needed it, but I don't think I could fight her again. Would I even have to? I'm not sure I would make it out alive.

"What happened to me? Where's the everfyre?"

Castiel tips his head and relief floods my body as I see the little blue flame flickering happily on a dusty chair. "Rowan carried you out of the cave. We figured something was wrong because you had been gone for so long, but once I saw you, I knew for sure that something wasn't right. You had those blue lines all over your body and wouldn't wake up." He gestured to the lines that covered my body and my face.

"Do... do you know what this is?" I whisper.

He shakes his head, and a pit grows in my stomach. "Freyin said nothing about poison..." I curl my hands into fists and stare at the crispy bird on the table.

"Who's Freyin?"

"What? Oh. The Elder One I had to fight to get this stupid everfyre." I turn around and grab the glass jar, relishing how solid it feels in my hand before placing it in front of us on the coffee table. It casts a blue glow against the reddish-orange skin of the roasted bird.

His brows raise. "An Elder One? You *fought* an Elder?"

"Yeah," I wave my hand. "It wasn't a fight to the death or anything... at least, I didn't think so. Now I'm not so sure."

"What kind of faerie is she?"

His question gives me pause. "I couldn't really tell. She had a white glow to her, and she stepped out of a white realm rather than the dark ones we step through when we realmwalk. Her hair was light and like mine, but her skin seemed almost translucent. Oh, and her hair had some sort of magic that turned it into a weapon."

We're silent for a moment.

"We really don't know very much about Elder Ones, do we?" He rubs the back of his neck.

I agree. None of us learned much about the Elder Ones from the old days. History isn't really taught to faeries; why learn about it when almost everyone who lived through it is still alive?

We seem to forget that history is important. Before we were divided into our own courts, we were united. Faeries all shared similar powers, with only a few having an affinity for certain elements. After the split, more faeries were born with powers from their court. My magic, if it weren't for my human blood, would glow darker and resemble the night sky with stars. Castiel's magic is warmer, marked golden with smears of yellow, orange, and red.

To this day, it's still unclear to us newer generation of faeries the entire story as to *why* Eldritch divided us into our courts. We know the the Dark fae committed treason and incited an uprising which brought about irreconcilable division, but no one talks about the truth of what actually happened. As punishment, all Dark fae were marked for their exile while Eldritch carved up the lands into what we now call our courts.

Though the Dark Court never settled on a monarch, they've been growing wilder and more chaotic. That's why it's so important that Elysia and Alfynia succeed in persuading my mother to open her court to others, and why I hope joining the Day Court will help our relations.

"Did you kill her?" He asks.

"No!" I gasp. "I said it wasn't a fight to the death. She used some intricate wording to imply I needed to kill her in order to win, but I have a feeling she was pleased I didn't go for death. I'm not sure that I would have succeeded, anyway. She is..." I pause, thinking of the right way to explain just how out of my league she was. "Freyin is faster and stronger than anyone I've ever met. I could barely defend myself for as long as I did, and I think I only got the upper hand because of the Vorukael's hint."

He raises a brow but says nothing.

We eat in comfortable silence for a while, which is odd for me. We haven't been stuck together for very long, especially considering how many years we spent at the Academy where he bullied me on the regular. And yet, the longer we spend alone, the more I realize that perhaps the Castiel I knew while growing up isn't the Castiel he truly is.

And I don't really know what to make of that.

"I treated your symptoms," he says without looking up. "You were in a lot of pain, and I couldn't pinpoint the source. All I could do was treat your symptoms and hope your body could fight it naturally."

I swallow before answering. "Thank you."

He doesn't respond for a moment. Instead, Castiel looks up. When we lock eyes, I see something I never thought would be directed at me in that sea of blue—dark in this moment with...

Regret. Remorse. *Anguish?*

"No," he shakes his head. "I should have been able to do more."

"How could you have?" I am careful with my words; I don't know how or *why* he's feeling this way. He kept me alive. That's more than anyone could have asked for.

His eyes flicker toward the windows, and a stream of light from the rising sun hits them in a way that highlights bits of gold I'd never realized were there.

"How are you feeling now?" He asks again, ignoring my question. I let it slide. He's opened up a lot in these past days, and I suspect it's more than he's shared with anyone in a long time. If he's not ready to talk, I don't want to force the issue.

"I'm better. I don't think there's going to be another attack..." I trail off, clenching and unclenching my hands. Everything feels fine to me, but what if it suddenly happens again?

"You haven't had one in over twenty hours. The interval between them has been increasing to the point where I have a feeling you might be out of the woods by now. I can barely see the lines anymore."

"You timed them?"

"Of course," he looks at me strangely. "How else would I have known whether your situation was declining?"

"I suppose that makes sense." Still, his diligence surprises me. Maybe he cares more about surviving and winning this challenge than I give him credit for.

"I have to head out and check my traps. I'll leave Rowan here with you in case anything happens." He stands up to leave, but I stop him.

"You should take Rowan with you—you don't know what's out there. Besides, I think I'm alright now." I want to go with him, but there are some things I want to explore in this cabin. Something about it piques my interest.

He stares at me for a long time before nodding stiffly.

"Let's go," he grabs the remaining food and calls out to Rowan. The giant wolf shakes his head and stands, padding silently across the cabin and following Castiel through the door.

As it closes, I feel a weight lift.

A TWIST OF NIGHT AND DAY

I need a moment to process everything that's happened.

The blue flame flickers in the little jar, reflecting a rainbow of lights as the sun hits it. I wave my hand over it. Dark blue sparkles engulf the entire jar before it all disappears; I've sent it to my reserve. Regardless of lesser or high fae, every faerie has one. It's a little like our own personal pocket in the Other Realm where we can store our things. It's not infinite, but the stronger the faerie, the more we can carry in our pocket realms. I usually fill mine with weapons.

I stand and look around the room, trying to distract myself from the spot of fear that threatens to take over my lungs and crawl up my throat. I see no reason why Freyin would not tell me about the poison unless she meant for me to die after our fight. No reason why she would poison me at all, especially after I'd defeated her.

Maybe I was wrong—maybe she did mean for me to kill her.

But these symptoms fade even as we speak. I can see the blue lines disappear from my hands with each passing minute. I'm sure that if I were to conjure a mirror, I could say the same for my face.

I feel fine now, and according to Castiel, I haven't had an attack in a long time.

Speaking of Castiel...

The couch beside me is cleaner than the rest of the cabin, except for the bed I slept in and the spot Rowan guarded. A blanket has been cast to the side.

Castiel slept here for the past three days—except for when he slept in the chair next to me.

The Castiel I knew and went to school with would have made a sly comment. He would have put me down in some way to make me feel like a burden, even though we're on this quest to get *his* throne back.

But this Castiel only seems regretful that he couldn't do more for me. And tired as he looks, he seems more relaxed than I'd ever see him. I almost suspect that with the first secret he revealed for the Vorukael, he started an avalanche of unveiling who he truly is on the inside; someone he'd kept hidden for so long because of the condemnation of his family and his peers.

And I don't know how to react to this Castiel.

Just because he has his problems doesn't mean he had the right to make others miserable.

I pick up a photo and clear off the dust with a wave of my hand and pause.

The magic that sprouts from my fingertips is not as dark as it normally is—flecks of white sprinkle throughout the darkness, broken by strands of silver highlighted by the sun.

I shake my head and return to the photo. It's of a faerie family from a long time ago—I can tell because the ears of the children are showing, and they're more rounded than ours.

Faeries from the old days were a lot closer to humans—there was more intermixing of races—and their ears weren't as pointed, just like with the Vorukael and with Freyin. At some point, faeries decided the mixing of races diluted our blood and made our magic less powerful, pulling away from mortals and condemning those who had anything to do with them.

The photo is a motion image, but the magic has faded with time without faeries around to charge it. A father and mother, both light haired, stand with their two children. The father holds a baby, while the other child stands in front of her parents and holds the mother's hand.

The image stutters. The daughter looks up at her mother with a hand in her mouth before dropping it and smiling at the camera.

Right before everyone stills for the moment the camera has captured, it stutters again and restarts, choppy.

Something squeezes in my heart, and I let my hand warm with magic to imbue the photograph with a little more time. Just because the people are no longer here doesn't mean the memories have to fade.

I reach for another photo, intending to recharge the magic in it as well when the surrounding air is slashed by a black tear.

Someone is realmwalking.

I open my hand and my sword appears in a small whirlwind of sparkles, settling solidly into my palm. A giant shadow bounds out from the inky depths.

Lowering my weapon, I reach to greet Rowan when he snaps at the air.

"What is it?" I ask, heart pounding when I realize Rowan would not have returned without Castiel unless something happened.

He growls low and angles his head toward his back. I take it as a sign to hop on and do so.

My legs are barely over his back when smoke and shadows rise from the ground, surrounding us in darkness. I blink and hear the temptations of the lost faeries, ignoring them over the thudding of blood in my ears. Shrugging them off, I cling onto Rowan's fur and urge him to go faster.

After what seems like too long, a rip opens in the darkness of the Other Realm and daylight peeps through.

Rowan charges at it, and we emerge to utter chaos in a small clearing in the woods.

CHAPTER TWELVE

MY HEART STOPS WHEN I realize what Castiel has stumbled upon.

A giant snake.

Its back faces me; the sun reflects a rainbow against its glittering deep purple scales as it sits half coiled, poised and ready to attack. Its underbelly is pure black except for a smattering of deep, blood red scales.

It is at least fifty feet long and thicker than the height of a fully grown faerie—even thicker than some of these ancient tree trunks. Its head is a rounded triangle with beady black eyes shining on each side. When it opens its mouth, two fangs longer and thicker than my forearms shine a terrifying white.

I call forth the jar of everfyre in one hand and my sword in my other. I've popped off the lid and am preparing to dip my sword in when I realize with pleasure that it's still lit from my bout with Freyin.

It takes a minute to pinpoint where Castiel is, but the direction that the giant snake is about to attack gives me a good hint.

I'm still on Rowan's back as he pads back and forth uneasily. His muscles ripple beneath my legs, coiled with tension. I glance to the tree that the Forescua Serpent is staring at—because there's no way this serpent is anything other than the Forescua—and it takes a minute, but I finally locate a flicker of blond hidden in between the branches and the leaves.

Imbuing some magic to my eyes, I squint through the glamor. Castiel's bleary form becomes visible through the leaves. He has his bow drawn and aimed, but he's too slow.

Horror pools in my stomach as the snake strikes first, snapping its jaws. I wince at the sound of the branches snapping from its massive teeth, but thankfully, Castiel's blond head jumps away at the last moment.

Unfortunately, he can barely hang onto the branch of the next tree with his bow in his other hand. Before I can react, he manages to pull himself up and nocks another arrow.

I need to do something soon. He can't keep hopping around.

I rearrange my grip and the everfyre seems to light up brighter. It might be my imagination, but the flames seem to flicker with more life, eager for what's to come. The Lunar magic in my sword thrums in my veins.

"Catch him when he falls," I whisper to Rowan before tucking the jar back into my pocket realm. I don't watch as it fades from view. I only keep my eyes on the Forescua.

The serpent's focus worries me; it turns its entire body toward the tree that Castiel is perched on and swings its massive head back and forth. Its forked tongue jumps out of its closed mouth, tasting the air, looking for the day princeling. I slide off Rowan and he immediately disappears into the shadows.

I calm my thundering heart and prepare myself for battle.

The serpent is huge, terrifying, and majestic. When it slithers on the ground, it makes no sound—probably dampened by magic. I can feel its brand of ancient magic spilling from its pores in waves, but I hope it doesn't have any hidden magical surprises like Freyin.

As the Forescua prepares to strike again, I cross the clearing silently, hoping what Freyin said about the everfyre's inextinguishable properties were right.

Its muscles coil, but I've already launched myself. I'm already in the air. I send a burst of magic to my feet right before I land—just in case its scales are as slippery as they look.

Hard beneath my feet, I realize with dismay that its scales are also sharp when I drop onto all fours. I struggle to cling on as it notices my presence on its back.

Before I can change my grip, the serpent thrashes. I should have expected this, but I didn't.

It flings me off.

Panic takes me for a moment as I fly through the air, but my instincts take over. My core tightens and I twist midair to land on my feet, my sword held out beside me to help with balance.

I wanted to distract its attention from Castiel, and I've succeeded.

The Forescua's beady eyes hone in on me and my heart thunders, but I'm also calmer than I've ever been. Combat is my element, and I revel in the adrenaline.

We stare at each other for a moment, and I wonder if it's intelligence or wickedness that I see in its eyes. Does it recognize the flame on my sword? Does it know I will be the one who kills it?

Its tail twitches, and I'm moving before I register what's happened. Instinct has taken over.

I rush at it. It lunges for me. Its mouth is wide open, its giant fangs glinting in the sun.

Right before we reach each other, an arrow ablaze with red-gold flames sails through the air and rips into the Forescua's mouth.

It closes its mouth and snaps the arrow in half, shaking with pain as smoke rises from the corners. While it's distracted, I take the opportunity to leap into the air.

I land directly on its head, as planned.

Knees bent and core tight, I fold myself over its head and grit my teeth against the pain of its sharp scales digging into my forearms. I barely stay on as it thrashes to throw me off, smoldering arrow forgotten already.

I shift my weight and let myself drop to sit closer on the back of its neck, clutching with my thighs to free my hands.

Its sharp scales dig into my legs and I clench my teeth, feeling the warmth of blood pour. I ignore the pain and hold on to my sword with both hands.

I am about to thrust its tip into the serpent's neck when I sense it tense differently, throwing me off balance so I have to take one hand off my sword and wrap my arm around its neck to hold on. I hiss as its scales dig into my exposed skin. I should have worn better armor.

Through the distracting pain, I realize with dread that the serpent can *spit*.

Somehow, it manages to shoot a purple glob with deadly accuracy, only barely missing Castiel as he springs from his branch.

The branch sizzles and falls to the ground with a thump as the brightly colored spit dissolves the wood.

Poison.

Castiel releases another flaming arrow, and the Forescua ducks at the last minute; the tip nearly hits me, singing a bit of my hair.

"Watch where you point that thing!" I yell.

"Don't get in the way!"

I growl and place both hands on my sword again, getting ready to plunge it into the thick neck.

But it's like the serpent can sense what I'm doing.

It bucks hard.

I curse; my thighs are slick with blood and I can feel its metallic scales dig through even more of my pants as I lose my grip. Cursing as I'm sent flying again, I ignore the burning in my legs as I twist in the air to avoid the glob of poison it shoots my way.

I land hard, gritting my teeth against the pounding that shoots up my legs. From my periphery, I see a black shadow launch itself at the snake's side.

Another three flaming arrows distract it while Rowan throws himself at the Forescua's neck.

Rowan's fangs sink into the serpent's neck and I charge at it from the side, my sword up in the air.

I thrust my blade into its long neck. The metal of my sword protests against the hard scales as it slices through the tiny shields until it reaches soft flesh.

I twist.

It lets out an unnatural roar and thumps its tail against the ground hard enough to uproot a nearby tree. I just hope Castiel isn't in it as it falls.

The Forescua foils my attempt at decapitation when it sends another cry into the sky and whips around faster than I anticipate.

I stumble and barely regain my footing, darting to avoid a quick attack by its tail. Rowan is on the other side of the clearing, shaking as he pushes himself up from the ground.

Fear grips my throat when I realize the blood that pours from its two wounds is already slowing.

It's healing.

My shredded legs start feeling like rocks as I realize its attention is focused solely on Castiel, who's raining a surprising assortment of arrows to provide us with time to recover. Some explode midair, blinding the serpent. Others split as they soar. Within his barrage of gold are a few scattered arrows wrapped in thicker, brighter red ropes. While the golden ones clink harmlessly against the serpent's metallic armor as a distraction, some of the crimson ones manage to pierce through, eliciting earth-shattering roars of pain from the beast.

They all hit their intended marks.

I meet Rowan's gaze and I know he understands me.

Pulling my sword close to my side, I charge. At the same time, Rowan rushes at the serpent.

But it seems to have decided it is most mad at Castiel and refuses to remove its beady eyes from him, even knowing that we're coming for him.

The Forescua whips its tail back and forth viciously, forcing me to back away first before pushing Rowan out of the clearing as well.

It charges at Castiel and spits several gobs of bright purple venom. I dart back and forth, but its whipping tail keeps us at bay.

I growl under my breath and change my tactic, heading toward the nearest tree. Clamping on the handle of my blade with my teeth, I try to ignore the burning in my legs as I make my way up the trunk, letting its boughs provide cover.

The serpent focuses on Castiel while Rowan fends off its thrashing tail.

Gauging the distance it'll take, I test the branch to see how far I can push my weight. Satisfied, I climb on and release the magic that's been burning under my skin. A silvery ball of fire forms in my palm, growing with each passing second. I silently urge it to grow faster; I don't know how much longer the two of them can dodge the serpent. Once it's about the size of my head, I aim it at the Forescua.

My fireball soars through the air soundlessly, but the explosion on impact is enough to distract it even if it does no harm.

Not before it spits another poisonous attack at Castiel.

The hairs on my neck raise when I hear his cry of pain.

Purple dribbles ominously from his right shoulder and his eyes are screwed shut. He drops his bow—I wave my hand to pocket it before it can fall and be crushed—as I launch from my tree toward him.

But in my periphery, Rowan does the same. I drop to the ground instead.

The serpent swings its massive head toward me, and all I hear is the pounding of blood in my ears as I come face to face with it.

I swallow and raise my sword.

Without hesitation, it dives, jaw dropping wide enough to swallow me whole.

Instinct takes over, and I thrust my sword up vertically. Its jaws clamp down on both ends of my sword and it flinches as the ancient metal coated with flickering blue flames burns the inside of its mouth.

I'm shocked that its giant fangs just miss me.

It backs away and hisses angrily, purple spit foaming at its mouth.

I dare to glance behind me and see Castiel on Rowan's back. His right arm is limp at his side, and purple bubbles horribly over his shoulder where the serpent's venom landed.

He's gesturing for me to come, but I lock eyes with Rowan.

Rowan understands.

Castiel's shout of displeasure rings through the forest loudly enough to catch the serpent's attention. It turns toward the princeling, but I sidestep and slash my sword against its back before hopping to the side.

Its murderous gaze swings to meet mine, flashing with anger and sinister vengeance.

The serpent's tail thumps angrily against the ground, shaking the entire forest floor.

Its jaws snap loudly at nothing as Rowan disappears into the rip in the fabric of reality while Castiel yells angrily through the void.

The tear closes, silencing his protests as Rowan realmwalks away with Castiel.

I hope he understood to come back for me.

"Just you and me," I whisper. I know it can understand me. The malice in that gaze is too intelligent for it not to.

Its obsidian eyes flicker to mine. Fury glitters in those black beads.

And maybe wickedness does, too.

My legs quiver, slick with blood. There's little hope of being able to climb back onto its back now that there are no distractions. I know my abilities, and I know I have a decent chance at killing it with a team.

Alone and injured? Maybe not.

I don't have the time to learn its maneuvers and its cues the way I want. It's all I can do to survive until Rowan comes back for me... if he comes back for me.

I let out a shaky breath and tighten my grasp on the handle. If I want to win, I should charge first and try to get the upper hand.

But I'm running low on energy and focus—and maybe blood, too.

And I'm worried about Castiel. I watched that purple poison dissolve branches thicker than a fully grown faerie like they were nothing. Only a splash of it touched his shoulder—but it's enough for me to worry about the state I'll find the princeling upon my return.

I stand my ground and dare the serpent to attack first. With a flick of its tail, the Forescua hisses and prepares to spit. I dodge to the right and curse as my knee buckles. I nearly lose my balance.

Without looking back at the spot that its poison hits, I can still hear the sizzle of the ground burning from its venom.

The Forescua eyes me with pure malice, and I wonder why it is such a hateful creature.

As I dodge again, I realize I would be angry too, if someone came to *murder* me while I was just minding my business.

Somehow, though, deep in my heart, I know that its anger is not directed solely at us. Yes, it was attacked unprovoked—but when I look into those black eyes, I know it is a hateful, angry creature at its core.

It hisses, purple frothing at its mouth. Its tail swishes back and forth in the air as it studies me. There is too much intelligence and emotion in its eyes; it looks more like a faerie that's taken the shape of the serpent and simply never changed back.

We dance back and forth. I do my best to avoid spending more energy than I can afford, hoping against all odds to figure out its pattern of attack and thoughts before—

My knees buckle. Its tail scrapes along my arm, taking with it my half-sleeve and a small length of unprotected skin. I involuntarily let go of my sword and it lands with a soft thud.

I lose all balance and fall, making sure to roll out of the way as its tail comes crashing back, leaving a giant dent in the dirt where I was just moments ago.

My entire right side burns even as I jump to stand. I cannot afford to lie around in pain.

I duck under some foliage and wordlessly focus magic on my shredded arm in hopes of staunching some of the bleeding. Panting hard, I peer out from behind a large drooping leaf, and see the hard purple glint of its scales as the serpent twists and turns, its forked tongue flickering to scent me.

My sword lays close to its belly—I can't recall it without alerting the serpent of my magic.

But I have no choice.

Swallowing my grunts, I pull myself up to lean against the tree trunk and make a fist to test my hand. It still aches, but at least it's usable.

The serpent flicks its tongue, tasting the air. Its beady, malevolent eyes search the forest for me.

"Here I am," I whisper. Tired of defending and frustrated with waiting, I charge. Pumping my legs, I jump into the air at the last second as it lunges toward me.

Its fangs dig into the ground, causing tremors that shake the surrounding trees. But I don't notice them—I'm entirely focused on my sword, which its gigantic, writhing body has knocked aside.

My blade fades out of existence and materializes in my hands, warm from the magic of being recalled. My fingers wrap around the familiar, solid hilt, and I swing it around in one smooth motion, pointing the tip at the back of the serpent's head as I drop.

The serpent is still busy trying to pull its fangs out from the earth as I brace for impact.

My feet slam against its hard scales, jarring me to the bones as I drive my sword as far as I can through its metallic armor. It roars with pain and bucks. I hang on for dear life, but my hands are slippery with its dark blood, sending me flying through the air. I try and flip to land on my feet but collide with the thick trunk of a tree instead.

I land on all fours, coughing up dirt and trying to catch my breath.

Groaning, and forcing myself up, I ignore the cuts on my palms and the heat spreading on my back from the harsh landing. My sword is still in the Forescua's neck as it thrashes wildly, spitting venom into the ground without direction in its fury.

At this point, I'll be torn to ribbons before Rowan returns.

I almost let out an audible sigh of relief when a familiar shadow tears through the air and a sleek black wolf jumps through.

In that moment, the Forescua rips up chunks of dirt from the earth and frees itself, spinning furiously enough to dislodge my sword. It probably sensed the magic of Rowan's realmwalking.

I gather the little energy I have left and aim it at my sword, which lies harmlessly on the ground surrounded by its blue flames. My blade raises with a twist of my wrist and points its flaming tip at the serpent.

The serpent's attention flickers toward it, and I catch the squint of its eye as it gets ready to attack.

Throwing my arm forward, my sword catapults and distracts the Forescua.

Rowan picks up on what I'm doing and leaps over, crossing the distance between us in two quick strides. I grab fistfuls of soft black fur and throw myself over his back. Wind and smoke surround us as Rowan jumps into the Other Realm.

As soon as the rip in the fabric of reality closes behind us and I hear the voices of the lost fae, I snap my fingers and pocket my sword, hoping the everfyre has not extinguished, but too tired to check.

I relax against Rowan's thick fur and let his heat soak into my weary body, feeling the immediate relief of releasing my magic on the sword. Moving items by magic alone is difficult enough for the most skilled warriors at their peak. If I had more energy, I'd be shocked that I was able to pull off that distraction while so injured.

I'll add that to the list of stuff I'll figure out once we're done with this ordeal.

CHAPTER THIRTEEN

I PACE THE ROOM FOR what feels like the hundredth time while the last dredges of daylight peer through the magical window panes.

Castiel has been groaning on the bed, slipping in and out of feverish consciousness for hours. I curse my rudimentary healing skills; I inelegantly stitched myself up, but I have no clue how to fix *him*. His wound is too advanced for my basic knowledge.

A bucket of water sizzles quietly beside the bed; I'd done my best to clean around the sickly poisoned skin, but the purple froth immediately burns away at anything that touches it. Any water I get on the wound also sizzles and evaporates instantly upon contact.

Rowan lays down next to the bed, his head resting on the mattress by Castiel's legs. He looks at me for answers I don't have.

Wait.

Answers.

The door slams behind me as I sprint outside; I don't even bother with gathering the necessary summoning items—I have a feeling the Vorukael wasn't trapped in my ash and iron circle at all, so there's no point in wasting time on things I won't even need.

The last time we summoned the Vorukael, Castiel's idea was to have me shoot him. It worked because of his secret obsession with me; having me then shoot and threaten to kill him *with his own bow* was entertaining enough for the Vorukael to show up.

I don't have such luxuries this time.

I stand in front of the cabin, wracking my brain for ideas. Minutes drag on for too long before I feel dumb and desperate standing on the grass by myself as the sun approaches the mountains, and a chill runs through the air.

Finally, I decide simply to speak to it. Maybe it's around and can hear me?

"Vorukael," I greet the open air. "Please come forth. I have questions again."

I wring my hands and shift my weight as my only response is silence.

Letting out a groan, I try again.

"Vorukael," I say. "The two faeries who brought you entertainment last time are in trouble. We need your help."

Nothing.

"Remember how amused you were?" I note with displeasure that my voice sounds precariously close to begging. "You thought it was hilarious for me to shoot him. I can't shoot him anymore if he's dead."

I scratch my head in frustration. The sun sinks further on the horizon, lowering beneath the mountains and blanketing the forest and our cabin in deep hues that remind me too much of Castiel's eyes and his magic. The thought that he might actually die roots itself deep in my heart and grips it with iron talons.

He can't die.

Not after all the torture he's put me through. He simply cannot die by another's hands after all those years. If he's going to die, it'll be by *my* hands.

He especially can't die now that I'm just peeling away the layers he's seemingly wrapped his true self in.

The longer I spent with him, the more I realize the Castiel at the Academy is nothing like who he is *now*—or maybe this is who he has always been. I might still want to wring his neck and throw him across a dense forest, but it is because of his personality and the things he says. Not because he's hurt me.

Because if I'm to be honest, he hasn't hurt me since we started this insane challenge—which isn't really saying much for regular folk, but for someone like him? It's extraordinary to witness. Maybe it's because we haven't spent *that* much time together. Maybe it's because he needs me to survive.

Or maybe it's because he's finally let go of some of his deepest secrets, and the death of his family—though painful—is a relief of the pressures they put on him and the ones he put on himself from the way they treated him.

It's like someone has dropped a bucket of ice water over my head when I realize something.

I haven't even thought about my fate if he were to die—I've concerned myself only with *his* wellbeing.

I groan.

It appears I may have grown to care for him without even realizing it.

As soon as the realization dawns on me, an inky tornado forms, tearing through the air. From the depths of those shadows steps the Vorukael in his odd, gliding way of moving.

I almost cringe at the obsidian eyes that peer through the tattered hood—they remind me of the Forescua's. Do all Elders have solid black or white eyes?

"You have called upon me once again," he says. The Vorukael's voice is as strange as it was the first time: all around me in the air, but also in my head.

I bite my tongue from offending him with a sarcastic remark.

"I need your help," I say. "I don't think I have any new secrets for you, but tell me what you want, and I'll keep my part of the bargain." Castiel kept me alive when he didn't know how to heal me. I owe it to him to at least try—even if it means striking a deal with the Vorukael.

His faceless head tilts as those eyes study me with a glint of amusement. I suppress a shudder.

"What do you need?" Its odd voice fills the air.

"Castiel's been hurt—we met the Forescua, but its venom has poisoned him, and I don't know how to fix it. I'm not good at healing." I clench my fists at my weakness. I'd never considered it a vulnerability before—I can stitch myself up well enough after a fight, but in facing the reality that Castiel might die because of my inability, I feel guilt.

"So, you were able to get the everfyre, then." His voice is laced with that of a thousand fae, but through it all, I can hear that he... is pleased? Why should he care whether we succeed? A trickle of fear makes its way down my spine.

Are there consequences he can see? Ones that we don't know?

"Yes," I answer impatiently. "But that's not the most pressing matter here. I'm afraid he won't make it through the night without help, but I don't know how to help him."

"The venom of the Forescua is fatal."

My heart drops.

"There must be a way," I let the desperation tinge my voice, not caring if he knew how I truly felt. "There has to be something I can do."

His head tilts the other way. "And what do you have that I desire?"

"Anything," I croak. "What do you want? I can get it for you."

"You know what I accept as payment." The Vorukael puts his hands together, touching only at the fingertips.

"I don't have any new secrets since we last met," I shake my head. "Are you sure there's nothing else you want? What about a favor?"

It stares at me silently for so long I worry my bottom lip. It's as if the Vorukael is reading me—looking right into my soul and figuring out if I'm worth the effort. I'm not comfortable feeling so bare and vulnerable, but I tell myself it's necessary if he can help Castiel.

"You have not yet discovered the only fun secret you bear." If someone can sound as though they're smiling, it's the Vorukael.

Panic courses through my body.

"Please give me a hint," I beg. "I can come up with something worthwhile."

The Vorukael shakes his head. "No, it's better this way. You'll figure it out later. You two have brought me much amusement, so I will allow you to pay me with a favor instead."

Relief floods me. "Great," I mutter. "What do you want? What can I do for you?"

His wind chime laugh resonates. "I will call on it at my leisure."

Ice spreads in my chest as a ball of dread grows deep in my belly. Owing a faerie is dangerous. It was bad enough that I offered a favor, but giving a faerie an open debt with no timeline as to when it can be collected is worse.

But I have no choice.

I swallow hard and nod.

He looks gleefully at me and I clench my jaw in fear as magic surrounds us. It's invisible, but I taste it on my tongue. It's not the same magic I'm used to. The bargain with the Vorukael isn't as metallic—it feels far older. Darker.

Wilder.

I only dare to breathe once the air returns to normal.

"The only way to cure Castiel of the poison is to destroy the Forescua's current body. Once it's gone, its hold over Castiel will end... assuming you can do it before he dies."

I gulp. "Is there anything you can do to help him? I just need a little more time..."

"It is already done," the Vorukael nods, almost in a bowing fashion. "He'll last at least another day, but not much longer than that. If you want to save him, you'll have to hunt the Forescua and break the curse tonight."

Relief washes over me—strong enough to momentarily forget the sacrifice I made. "Thank you," I say.

"Be aware," the Elder whispers in my mind as it fades. "The Forescua is not what it seems to be."

I almost snort but refrain from doing so in case he finds it offensive. There is no doubt about that—I've been worried about what else it might have up its figurative sleeve on top of its deadly venom. The Vorukael would have been much more helpful if he'd just *told* me what else that serpent can do.

It looks like a terrifying giant snake and is as formidable as one would expect—what more could it be hiding?

The Vorukael fades out of existence as the moon begins its ascent. The forest returns to life as if nothing happened at all. As if I didn't potentially sign my life to an Elder.

Another day's problem.

I rush back into the cabin as darkness falls. As soon as I enter, I know something has changed.

Rowan is pacing back and forth, his giant body making it difficult for him to turn, but he does so anyway.

Castiel sits up on the bed, his cheeks flush with fever. He rubs the back of his neck and blinks hard at his surroundings. One hand reaches out for Rowan, who stills immediately. Castiel doesn't look well, but he's at least conscious and lucid.

"Glad you didn't die on me," I say calmly despite squashing the blossoming urge to lean forward and hug him. The rush of relief gives me pause, and I don't want or need him knowing.

"You'll have to try a little harder," he smiles wryly.

"You might be more trouble than you're worth," I force a smile. "I had to summon the Vorukael for help."

Castiel stiffens. "The Vorukael? What did you give in return? I can't believe I missed your secret after you heard mine." His brow furrows, his voice rough with sleep. Though he's awake, I can see the strain his body is under. His gaze is unsteady, and his eyes are tinged with red. His cheeks bloom with an unnatural rosiness.

I hesitate. "I didn't have to give a secret; he said that you amused him so much he didn't mind answering my question." I don't know why, but it makes me uncomfortable to withhold the whole truth from him.

"At least mine was interesting enough to last two questions, I guess," he grumbles, then narrows his eyes. "What *else* did you give him?"

I shift under his critical gaze. Has he always been this shrewd?

"A favor," I mumble.

"A *what?*" His glare intensifies and my heart stumbles a little.

"You were dying," I cross my arms. "*Still* dying."

He mutters something incomprehensible before his shoulders droop in a sign of resignation as he winces. "What did you ask the Vorukael?"

I look at him pointedly before rolling my eyes. "I asked for the secret recipe to faecakes. What do you think I asked about? How to heal that, of course." I wave my hand at his shoulder, which is bubbling less, but still more than I'd like.

"And the answer?"

I bite my lip and look away, but he deserves to know the truth. "You'll die unless we can kill the Forescua tonight."

Rowan stills, a low rumble rising from his chest. Castiel doesn't seem worried considering *his* life is on the line.

"That works out for us all, then."

"What?"

"Well, I'm dead either way if we don't kill it. This just adds a little more urgency. How much time do we have before you're stuck as queen of your own court?"

I look at him, exasperated. "Are you serious?"

He shrugs.

I'm shocked at how little he values his life, but that's a discussion for another time. "We have less than a day before your condition… worsens."

"We should head out, then."

My jaw drops. "You're not coming. Rowan and I are going, but you have to stay here. Where it's *safe*."

"I might die either way."

"You're in no condition to fight!"

"I can serve as distraction, then." He grins cheekily, and I can feel my heart constrict against my will. "I wasn't doing much before, anyway."

I cross my arms. "You'll end up distracting *me*."

"So, you care that much about my wellbeing?"

I arch my brows.

"I'll stay out of sight."

"This is not a negotiation," I say dully.

"You're right," he responds with a quirked eyebrow. "It's not. It's my life, and I'm coming whether you like it or not."

I see the determination in his eyes. I see the rebellious nature and the need to do this. He's been controlled his whole life, and now his life might end before the day is over.

He needs to do this.

He needs the choice.

"Besides," he tilts his head up. "If you leave without me, I'll just realmwalk and end up with the lost fae, and then you'll lose your claim to be the Day King's Enforcer, anyway."

"Why would—" I stop when he looks at me sharply, brows raised with that signature half smile on his lips, and I suddenly understand. He can't realmwalk not because he physically cannot perform the magic, but because the pull of the lost fae is too strong.

He doesn't have much will to live. His friendships are shallow. His family neglects him. He doesn't have a personal desire to be king except for the inherent one placed on him by the land. He amuses himself with the suffering of others to numb his hatred of himself. It's hard not to give in to the temptations of the lost ones in that state of mind.

"Fine," I mutter, barely believing the words coming out of my mouth. "You can come, but you have to *stay put*."

He grins lazily.

"No jumping around like you were before. No getting within range of that venomous spit. Stay out of sight, and *don't you dare get killed*," I hiss.

CHAPTER FOURTEEN

WE RISK REALMWALKING again because there isn't time to spare, and I have a firm grip on Castiel's arm. He looks at my death grip—likely to leave a bruise—but doesn't complain. The whispers fade with the darkness, and we emerge from the Other Realm away from where we last encountered the serpent. Castiel rides on Rowan as I walk alongside them.

The moonlight does nothing to calm my nerves this time, and the cold doesn't seem to affect Castiel at all. His eyes shine with fever and pieces of his hair stick to his forehead.

I worry we're running out of time.

My heart pounds at the memory of the last time we were in this part of the woods. I was unprepared then. I've since replayed the scenario a thousand times in my head, planning my moves. Knowing we cannot fail.

I'm glad Rowan's realmwalking deposits us farther than where we need to be, because I don't know where the serpent might be hiding. I didn't see a cave or a burrow earlier today—maybe it's too large to sleep anywhere but in the open. Any creature would have a death wish if it were to disturb the Forescua.

I nearly snort; no wonder Ryken sent us on this quest.

A TWIST OF NIGHT AND DAY 169

The wind shifts. I freeze.

Rowan twists his large body behind a tree, pressing Castiel into it. Castiel grunts and slides off; a warm glow by his arms signaling his bow being called from his reserve.

The princeling leans heavily against the thick trunk but straightens when he notices my worried gaze, pulling a lazy smirk onto his face as though the moonlight doesn't make him paler and more sickly looking.

Rowan steps up to my side and peers at me with one silver eye that looks white against the light. I nod tersely and pull myself onto his back in one smooth motion. My legs and my core automatically stiffen, familiar by now with this position.

"Stay *here*," I hiss at Castiel's faint silhouette.

"Thanks for worrying about me." He waves a hand nonchalantly, and I look over warily as he makes his way clumsily up the tree. I swallow a lump in my throat and can't help but notice how difficult his movements seem now compared to his fluid motions just earlier in the day.

Even injured and feverish as he is, he still makes quick work of the climb and reaches the top faster than I expected. A quick glamor later, I lose sight of his blond head as he blends in with the shadowy forest.

Satisfied, I tap Rowan's side with my knee, and we prowl.

Again, I'm impressed by Rowan's ability to move both effortlessly and silently given his mountainous size. I shouldn't be surprised—he is a predator, after all.

The moon's glow breaks the forest's shadows with streaks of silver and white, but the giant wolf has no problems maneuvering between the swaying branches. It's almost as if the forest parts for him, knowing he's from the Other Realm and fearing his presence.

Something catches his eye, and he turns so sharply I almost fall off. After a moment of disorientation, I see the hard purple glint.

I hardly dare to breathe as Rowan slows and lowers into a crouch.

The serpent lays asleep, coiled around itself in an open area not far from where we retreated. Its thick muscles relax as it breathes. The tip of its tail flicks, and we stop in our tracks despite being far enough that it can't possibly scent us.

I hope.

Rowan takes us quietly around the clearing's edge so we can survey the scene.

Dried blood—my blood—dull the colors of its sharp scales. A trail shows where I slid along its back.

I'm glad I had the foresight to wear better protection this time around.

My sword is strapped to my back, blue flames still licking at the steel. The everfyre, as I discovered, reacts to my thoughts. If I don't actively wish for it to harm something, I can even lay my sword down on the forest floor without the grass catching on fire.

I just hope it can seal the Forescua's neck once I slice through it—I grimace at the thought of having to face *two* heads.

I hop off Rowan's back and we split up. He takes one side of the clearing, and I take the other.

We're still getting into position when a twig snaps—I freeze.

Who?

I don't know how it's possible, but my already rapidly pounding heart beats faster. I look frantically across the field and meet Rowan's equally harried silver eyes.

The Forescua stirs.

I pull a small dagger from my boot. The forest floor seems empty, but I look anyway hoping to silence whichever creature might wake the serpent and disrupt our plans.

Silently cursing when nothing catches my eye, Rowan and I both stay still and wait for the Forescua to fall back asleep.

Thankfully, it doesn't take long before its swollen midsection rises and falls rhythmically again.

I continue making my way around the clearing, staying as quiet as possible.

As we settle into place, the wind changes.

I blink, and I'm suddenly looking into a beady, obsidian eye glowing with hatred.

It breathes hard through its nose. Warm, rancid air brushes against my face. I don't dare to blink again.

Does it see me?

I hold my breath as its eyes run along me...

... and it continues on.

Something clicks in my head: *it doesn't see stationary things*—not close up, anyway. That gives me an idea.

As soon as its head swings away toward Rowan, I move.

I wish I could have used magic to dampen the sounds of my footsteps, but I have a feeling the Forescua is even more attuned to magic than it is to sound.

Darting along the forest floor, I am hyper aware of what's around me. The serpent continues threading its head back and forth around an invisible obstacle course visible to no one else.

Another twig snaps and everyone freezes.

I quiet my breathing and look around—*what is making that noise?*

If it's Castiel, I will *kill* him.

Thankfully, I don't see him even around the tops of the trees. If he gets too close, the Forescua might sense his invisibility glamor.

All at once, it's as if the entire forest wakes up.

Birds I didn't know were in this forest caw.

A mass of glittering black-violet charges. Two enormous white fangs barrel toward me.

All conspicuity gone, I duck and roll just in time for those giant jaws to snap a thick tree trunk in half. The sound is even more thunderous knowing that it could have been my small body between those deadly jaws.

Without a hitch, its head turns to me and its entire body moves faster than I have seen it before. It's slithering to me, chasing me. Angry.

I run.

There's no use trying to be quiet now—it has its sights set on me. Hopping over a felled log, I turn mid air and send silver-white fireballs from my free hand.

I don't bother to aim, wanting only to slow it down so I can figure out my next move.

From the crackling and hissing behind me, I can tell it's having trouble catching up through the fireballs. Sending some magic to my feet, I jump and land on the treetops in one leap.

Shooting more fireballs as I turn, I aim for the sounds of its thick serpentine body crushing the forest floor.

A few hit their targets, but they are only nuisances for its sharp-scaled body. It shakes its gigantic head and blinks away the remaining embers, hissing with rage.

I launch from my perch.

The thump of my feet on its razor-sharp scales brings a shiver up my back; my legs remember how sharp the scales are as I drop to mount it. I'm glad I had the foresight to wear my leathers this time.

It thrashes in a wild fury; its tail sends vibrations through the ground, felling trees. It hisses as it turns to attack, letting out an unnatural growl when it realizes it can't reach me where I'm perched on its back.

My core tightens, and I hope the extra magic I've sent to my legs is going to keep me hanging on for longer. I shimmy farther up its neck with one hand and hold my sword in the other, afraid I won't have time to pull it out quickly enough if I store it.

I wince. A scale cuts through the leather that wraps around my arm. A quick whispered charm beneath my breath and the blood that seeps out is wicked away; I've learned from last time. I can't risk losing too much.

As I look up, something hits me in the head and sends me flying from its neck. I drop my sword in the process.

The breath is knocked from my lungs as I land hard on my back. Branches that dig into my spine are nothing compared to the pounding in my head.

Stars block my vision.

I squeeze my eyes shut and shake my head only to groan out loud from the ringing.

Through blurred vision, a shadow appears.

I wrap my hands around my head and roll to get up just in time as its tail slams against the earth.

My knees buckle, and I'm on the ground again.

Gasping for breath, I push back into a standing position.

A dark blur darts back and forth in front of the Forescua. Rowan distracts it so I can recover.

Sending some magic to my head, I sigh as most of the throbbing subsides and I can see clearly again—just in time to watch as the serpent flicks its tail into Rowan and throws the wolf into a tree.

My turn.

Retracting the magic from my head and pouring it into my legs instead, I leap into the sky. Soaring through the air is exhilarating as I hold my sword with both hands, aiming the tip down as I tuck my limbs in and drop like a rock.

The serpent senses my magic and twists as I approach.

I land on the middle of its back instead of its head.

It lets out a guttural roar as deep purple blood pours.

The Forescua bucks, but I grab on, ignoring the sharp edges of its scales against my skin. My crimson blood mixes with its violet, but I feel nothing as adrenaline pumps through my body.

Reaching into my boot, I pull out a small dagger.

I try to jam it into the Forescua as a handhold, but the blade only bounces back, sending tremors through my hand. Frustrated, I shake my hand out and discard the knife. From

A TWIST OF NIGHT AND DAY

the angle I straddle the snake, there's no way I can use my sword instead.

But the serpent is shaped so that it's thinnest at its neck and tail. Maybe I can get close enough to the neck to sever its head from there.

Rowan darts back and forth before the serpent. The wolf is more majestic than any creature I'd ever seen; if I hadn't known he was of the Other Realm, I'd have definitely suspected it from watching him in battle. He moves so quickly that he often is no more than a black blur as he seeks for an opportunity to sink his teeth in the serpent's soft underbelly.

Instead of twisting into knots chasing the wolf, the Forescua stays in one spot and focuses on spitting its poisonous venom, making it easier for me to climb its scales without being noticed.

When I finally reach its head, I slash downwards, gritting my teeth from the feeling of my ancient sword forcing its way through the primordial scales.

Its roar reverberates throughout the forest. It thrashes so hard I lose grip and sail through the air. Rowan catches the back of my shirt with his teeth and drops me gently, saving me from another rough tumble.

I nod gratefully.

He blinks before turning his silvery gaze back to the thundering snake.

My sword still sticks in the serpent's side.

I open my palms and summon it back, which attracts the serpent's attention. The hatred in its eyes is enough to take my breath away. It whips its tail at us, fervent and almost frothing at the mouth with rage.

Rowan darts away in time, but I stumble.

Its tail feels like solid steel as it collides with my side, throwing me across the clearing.

A small tree snaps in half, cracking against my battered body.

I can barely breathe. I don't know how far I've fallen. It's been a long time since my body has taken such a beating.

Seconds feel like hours as I groan, trying to pull myself up. All I achieve is rolling onto my side.

Faerie bodies are sturdier than those of humans, but not by much. While I survived the impact, my entire body roars with bone searing pain. A fresh wave of agony rips through me each time I try to move.

Something bubbles in my throat, and I cough out blood. It's so painful I almost lose consciousness.

I hear a rustle too close for comfort, but it hurts too much to turn. I have to get back to Rowan; he can't fend the snake off forever.

I stare at the heavy forest canopies. I can't tell if the sky is darkening or if I'm losing consciousness.

A rough male voice curses beside me, but my mind is so foggy it takes a minute to realize it's Castiel. Painstakingly, I turn my head even though I still can't see him. His invisibility glamor is still up, but it's better this way. He's safer.

I want to tell him to keep the glamor on, but my breaths are quick and shallow—and it's getting harder with every passing moment. Speaking isn't even an option.

I don't see his hands, but I can tell where they are from the golden flames that flicker to life. The warmth caresses my chest, warming my ribs. The heat reaches around my body to my back and I swallow a cry when I feel my bones reset.

My mind clears from the fog of pain as the magical sparkles rove down my legs. Tingles follow the glowing shower as my broken body heals.

The sensation grows as I bite my lip and squeeze my eyes shut, tears leaking anyway through the torturous healing process as the worst of my gashes stitch themselves up once all my bones are back in their places.

I can almost see Castiel's concentrated face as his hands hover, magic pouring from his palms and fingertips.

This is both far more advanced and efficient healing than I could do, and as my thoughts clear, I'm suddenly grateful for him having broken my rule of not moving from his spot.

When he's fixed my right arm, I flex both hands to test it out.

"Thank y—"

A yelp snaps my attention back to the clearing.

"Don't expose yourself," I warn him quickly before getting up and returning to battle, ignoring the residual aches.

Castiel healed the gravest of my injuries, but I am still bruised and battered. Nothing works quite as it should, but I can still do this.

I have to do this.

Rowan struggles to stand, shaking his head. The Forescua slithers toward him like it knows it's won.

Willing my legs to move faster, I cross the field in a matter of moments. In another heartbeat, I'm looking up at the snake's chin.

The pebbled scales reflect white in the moonlight, rounded rather than sharp.

I thrust my sword upward with all the energy I can muster.

The blue flames flicker to life, leaping toward the Forescua's soft, exposed underside like they know exactly where to go.

It tries to look down, but flaming arrows hurtle up ahead and whiz past its eyes. It snaps left and right, dragging me and my sword with it.

I hang on for dear life as it tosses me about. This is my chance, and I will not squander it.

Tightening my core and straining, I heave myself up and wrap my legs around its neck. I dangle upside down while white-knuckling the hilt of my sword.

Wind whips against my face as the Forescua throws its entire body back and forth in an effort to dodge Castiel's flaming arrows and Rowan's sharp teeth. The reverberations of its roars rock me to my very core.

But at least it's too distracted to focus on me.

Clenching my teeth, I shimmy down its neck and pour magic into my arms so I have the strength to yank the sword down its throat as I move.

The serpent's roaring turns to howls as its movements grow wilder with panic. Thick, purple blood gushes out, coating my arms.

The arrows don't cease, and Rowan moves so fast he's a blur of shadows.

Its struggling suddenly slows—not by much, but it's enough.

Again, I gather all my strength as I shuffle lower down its body.

A TWIST OF NIGHT AND DAY

I push the sword deeper into its neck until I feel its flesh press up against the hilt and against my hand; its blood drowns my hands and makes it harder to keep my grip.

I wrench my sword downward.

I do this again and again until I'm so low on its neck that I fear its body will slam me into the ground with one wrong move.

Finally, I let myself drop as it hisses with pain, slowing even more.

My feet land solidly against the ground, though my arms quake with exertion.

The serpent moans and I recognize the twitch in its eye as it's about to spit its deadly venom.

With a heave, I pour what little magic I have left into my arms and—for good measure—into my sword as well.

A vicious, unrecognizable war cry leaves my lips, and I throw my arms upward and over in an arch. Grunting as my sword makes contact, my arms protest at the resistance.

My steel sings as its ancient metal slices through the Forescua's deadly scales.

I push forward.

Living blue flames meet the dark purple body like engulfing smoke.

Welcoming it.

Greeting it.

Saying goodbye to it.

Blue and purple become one as I push and push until finally, the thrashing and roaring and hissing stops. The sea of gushing purple blood turns into a sputtering stream.

A dull thud sounds, but I barely hear it.

My arms are as numb as my mind.

I'm covered with sticky, purple blood, and a lot of the injuries Castiel healed have opened again. I don't feel the impact as my knees hit the hard forest floor.

The serpent lays lifeless beside me, its black eyes smoking over and turning grey. A little venom dribbles from its fangs, but the stump of its neck has cauterized as I'd hoped.

I shift away from it despite my body feeling heavier than I ever remember. I end up rolling clumsily.

My ears still thunder from the adrenaline and my heart still pounds like it's trying to escape my chest. I swallow thickly and look to the trees where Castiel must be perched, keeping an eye on the serpent in my periphery. I'm not sure I believe that it's really dead, but I understand why the Forescua's thrashing slowed—its tail is pinned to the ground by a thick arrow that's smoking blue as the flames fizzle out.

The air shimmers, and Castiel's body slowly reveals itself from the glamor.

He hops effortlessly down from his branch and comes running over, though his footsteps sound oddly muffled.

I think everything is muffled, because he looks like he's yelling something—except I don't hear anything.

Suddenly, I'm lifted and tossed aside like a sack of rocks. Grunting in protest, I push myself up from the ground, still bleary from the fight.

Castiel kneels next to me, his hands hovering over my body as warm, golden flames leap from his hands.

Rowan crouches and growls low in his chest, standing over us protectively.

Alarm bells peal loudly in my head. *Something is wrong.*

I muster what little energy I have left and focus on the corpse of the Forescua...

... only to watch it light up in purple and black flames. Its entire head and body are separately engulfed in a bright, violet tornado. The force of the heat that blasts from the dark whirlwind nearly pushes me back. It dies down to reveal the body of a male faerie panting hard on his hands and knees.

CHAPTER FIFTEEN

WE GAPE AS THE REST of the flames fade, leaving behind piles of ashes where the serpentine body and decapitated head used to lie.

The male that remains has alabaster skin and black hair falling over his eyes. He's dressed in all black.

My heart stops when he looks up.

I know those purple eyes.

Those are the same eyes as the faeries who sit on Castiel's throne.

The same eyes as the faeries who sent us on this crazy Challenge.

Those are the eyes of Euphelia and Ryken.

How is this possible? How does this faerie have their eyes? Their hair and their noses? Who is he?

Before we can react, the stranger pulls himself upright. Dark patterns—the mark of Dark faeries' exile—flicker on his neck. Panting hard, he draws a massive amount of crackling black and purple flames between his hands. He looks up at the dark sky and drags his eyes to us. He raises his hands and launches the angry fireball.

It hurtles toward us at speeds I can't comprehend. Before I can react, a giant orange and gold circle spreads in front of us just in time. White explodes as the black ball of flames collides with Castiel's shield.

The golden prince's arms are up; his heels dig into the ground, jaw clenched in concentration. Sweat forms on his forehead as he pushes forward.

The mysterious Dark faerie prepares for a second attack. I push myself up and muster up what little magic I have left. My silver-blue shield appears, joining the orange-gold one of Castiel's.

The stranger's second attack is much smaller, exploding on contact with our magical shields and shattering into a million little pieces.

By the time the smoke clears and our shields come down, the stranger is nowhere to be seen.

A vicious wind blows through the clearing, lifting ash and blocking our vision. A rush of fear spreads in my veins as I realize I've over-extended my magic.

"What—" I start to ask, but black spots appear in my eyes. The world spins, and then nothing.

I WAKE TO RAIN PATTERING against the cabin's familiar log roof.

Had I dreamed the fight with the Forescua?

I couldn't have—my body hurts too much.

The aches are too deeply rooted to be healed by magic. It's the type of ache you can only recover from if you get enough rest.

Rowan whines low, and Castiel is by my bed before I can blink.

"Hey," he says. His light blue eyes are soft, and it makes me uncomfortable in a way I can't quite explain.

"Hey," I try not to warm under the heat of his stare.

"I feel like we're doing this too often," he grins weakly, rubbing the back of his neck.

"How are you?" I stare pointedly at his shoulder to avoid eye contact.

He chuckles. "How am I? How are *you*?"

"I'm fine. How much time has passed? Are you still—?" I try and gesture to his shoulder but wince instead.

He raises a hand like he is about to touch my face, but he lets his hand float in the air before making a fist and dropping it.

I pretend not to notice.

"You killed the Forescua, so I'm fine. But you lost consciousness right after that faerie appeared from the ashes of its corpse."

I freeze as memories of violet eyes and glittering hatred resurface.

"Who was that?"

He shrugs. "I don't know. But seriously, how are you?"

"Seriously, I'm fine," I mimic him.

He glares, but there isn't any bite in his eyes. "For 'the best warrior of our generation,' you sure are losing consciousness a lot."

My brows furrow. "This isn't normal for me."

"I was teasing you," his voice softens further. "You fought two Elders and lived to tell the tale. These aren't exactly normal situations."

My shoulders relax. "Did you notice his eyes?"

His navy-blue eyes darken. "You mean how he looked like Euphelia and Ryken?"

I nod.

"They have some explaining to do, don't they?"

I SPEND HALF THE DAY resting at Castiel's behest. I told him I felt fine, but he was relentless in his insistence that I should sleep to recover from the aches that his magic couldn't heal.

I will not admit to him he was right; the extra hours accelerate my healing. By the third time I wake, I feel like a brand-new person.

We make a beeline out of the Lunar Courts on Rowan's back. I was apprehensive at first when he motioned for me to sit in front of him, but when I settled into his arms, I pushed all those uncomfortable thoughts away.

There are other more important things to think about before we face the siblings again—such as who the mysterious Dark faerie is and whether the dark siblings knew he would emerge from the Forescua's body.

I don't have time to think about trivial things such as Castiel's solid front against my back as Rowan trots through the Courtless.

Just as we don't know much about Elder Ones, the Dark faeries are also mostly a mystery—especially to us, the newer generation of faeries. We still don't know why Euphelia and Ryken murdered the Ares family and took over the Day Court.

The Dark Court operates differently; they've never had a proper king or queen, meaning the faeries are as wild as the land. The Lunar Court is a testament—a warning—to what would become of the Day Court if we let them take over.

But if this Dark faerie is their brother, does that mean Euphelia and Ryken are Elders?

No. That's impossible.

Neither siblings looked nor sounded like Freyin or the Vorukael. When I stood before the Elders, I could feel in my bones how ancient they were. I could hear the voices of thousands of fae behind theirs and feel the weight of thousands of years in their presence.

The Forescua couldn't talk, so I couldn't hear it's voice. But something doesn't feel right. It takes me a moment before it hits me.

I didn't feel the same ancient aura around the serpent as I did with Freyin and the Vorukael.

So, perhaps neither the Forescua nor the dark siblings are Elders.

But the Vorukael can only speak the truth—

What was it he said the last time I summoned him?

"The Forescua is not what it seems to be."

Before I have time to ponder further, we approach the sunny gates of the Day Court.

In just a week's time, the gates have drastically changed. Castiel stiffens behind me as he catches sight of the Dark faeries guarding the doors.

We slide off Rowan, who enters alongside us.

The guards are dressed in Dark Court garb. Their armor is all black and void of color—a contrast to the bright sun beating down on them and the pearly white and gold castle they protect.

"The wolf does not enter." One guard blocks our path with his sword, his exile mark prominent on the exposed pale skin of his hand and neck.

Both wolf and prince let out a savage growl, and the guard blinks hard.

"This is still *my* Court," Castiel snarls. "And I will bring whoever I choose into *my Court*."

The guard falters at the ferocity in Castiel's voice, and I must admit that for a moment, I'm brought back to the days of the Academy when he used those tones with me.

Castiel does not wait; he saunters toward the gate, expecting his command to be obeyed.

The guard's eyes dart from Castiel to his partner, but finally relents when his partner is too cowardly to speak. I don't have to see Castiel's face to know there is a haughty smirk plastered on it.

The three of us enter, and I realize Castiel has placed the mask of his old self back on. He slides into this persona so effortlessly and smoothly that I barely noticed it has happened. Maybe it is because he is not directing this ferocity at me.

Or perhaps he has played this part for so long that there is no distinction between this vicious, ruthless golden prince and the gentler one that I traveled with. Perhaps they have both become equal parts of who he is.

I envy his confidence.

Even if it's false confidence—even if he is quaking inside—I don't think I would be able to exude such arrogance and certainty. There is a strength in that ability—one which I lack. I may have the gall to face the Vorukael, Freyin, and even behead the Forescua, but I don't think I have the courage it takes for a deposed prince to strut back into his court and stake claim on his throne.

Not after his entire family was murdered.

We step into his palace side by side. He doesn't bother to give any guards or staff the time of day—not even a flicker of his gaze.

He doesn't have to.

Rowan, in my periphery, pulls his lips up at every Dark faerie we see.

We enter the throne room. It is empty and cold—an echo of what it was just a week ago. I try not to let my gaze linger on the checker-patterned floor where most of the Ares family was slain, though not a drop of blood remains.

The remnants of the glass panes in the giant windows have been removed, leaving the entire room open to the elements. Neither the cracks on the throne nor the walls have been repaired, and overgrowth has started taking over.

Thorny vines crawl up the walls, decorated by a smattering of flowers ranging from every shade of purple.

The faint click of heels sounds from across the room.

Euphelia enters from the doors on the other side, her chin up. Her lips are painted as bright red as I remember—as are her nails.

She's shed the enormous black gown for a simpler dress, equally bare of color. When she walks, the black cloth shimmers and fades into different shades—not plain grays, but charcoal, ebony, jets, and obsidians I hadn't known existed until this moment.

Behind her struts her brother.

Ryken looks as unruffled as ever. He, like his sister, is dressed in all black. The top buttons of his shirt are undone, and his pants appear custom tailored for his body. His black hair is slicked back, and his violet eyes study us with a modicum of surprise.

Euphelia takes a seat on the cracked throne and Ryken leans casually against its back.

"I have to say, I'm impressed." Ryken's deep voice resonates in the empty throne room. "We thought you'd give up much earlier than this."

Castiel rolls his shoulders and studies the taller faerie. "You make a lot of assumptions."

"Oh?" Euphelia rests a chin on her hand.

"We've defeated your serpent," Castiel tilts his head up. "And I've come to reclaim my throne. I hope you've kept it warm for me."

Blood pounds in my ears, and I don't miss the moment of shock that slips through their perfect facades of nonchalance.

Ryken recovers quickly.

"You've beheaded the serpent? But where is the head?" Ryken makes a show of looking left and right before clicking his tongue. "You know that lies and deception will not make it past the magic of Challenges."

"She beheaded it, but its corpse turned to ashes. We were wondering if you knew anything about that," he asks with an accusatory tone and narrowed eyes.

I resist the urge to wipe my sweaty palms against my pants. I don't like this spotlight, but my instinct says something bad is going to happen—especially when I notice the pale siblings whiten even more as the blood drains from their faces.

Ryken's eyes narrow. "You shouldn't lie," he hisses.

"We're not lying," I declare. I resist wincing as my sharp voice reverberates in the empty hall, sounding thin and uncertain.

"So, she speaks," Euphelia snarls.

They're shocked and angry—but most importantly, they're afraid. She's redirecting the conversation.

And for some reason, that stirs an inexplicable dread within me, too.

"You didn't bring its head back, so you don't get your wish," Euphelia waves her hand, feigning indifference and expertly masking her fear once more.

But I can see through their facades.

An odd rage swirls in my blood. There is something they're not telling us—something integral to our hunt for the Forescua. They weren't expecting us to succeed, not because of our skill, but because of *something else*.

Something they're not telling us.

"We beheaded the Forescua like you asked," Castiel says through gritted teeth. "You gave us the Challenge, and we completed it."

"No," Ryken looks down his nose at us. "Our Challenge was for you to *bring his head back*. Defeating him was only the obvious path to beheading the beast."

Him?

I start to protest, but he interrupts me.

A TWIST OF NIGHT AND DAY 191

"If, by some wild magic, the serpent were still alive even as you carried his head here, you would have succeeded. Death was not a requirement. The head was."

Castiel's eyes flash with a deadly blue as dark as midnight; his hands ball into fists at his side.

My breath comes in shallow bursts as I recall our last conversation here; Ryken is right. They told us to bring the head, but we have arrived empty-handed.

"You gave us an impossible task," I glare at Ryken's violet eyes, hoping my breath and voice are steady. "You *knew* we wouldn't be able to behead it because its body would turn to ash."

To my surprise, Ryken's eyebrows shoot up. "I can assure you that those were not the doubts we had regarding your success in this trial."

"What were they, then?" The savagery of my snarl shocks even me, but Castiel stays silent.

"The Forescua has no equal. His—"

"Did someone step out of the serpent's body?" Euphelia interrupts her brother, voice higher than I'd ever heard.

All eyes snap to her.

"Did someone *emerge from the serpent's body*?" Her already shrill voice raises another octave.

My blood heats.

I see red.

They *knew*.

They knew that someone was in there; they knew that it was impossible for us to get its head. The Vorukael's words pound in my mind as loudly as my heart pounds in my chest.

"The only way is to break the Forescua's current body."

"You'll have to hunt the Forescua to break the curse."

I had thought the Vorukael's wording was odd, but I chalked it up to his age; sometimes the older fae speak differently. But I see now the Vorukael was trying to warn me. The curse it spoke of was not the venom with which Castiel was poisoned.

He meant the *Forescua* was cursed—someone else lived in its body.

My head spins.

That's why the serpent didn't feel like an Elder.

Whoever the serpent was, that Dark faerie was the one controlling its body. It might have once been an Elder One, but it wasn't when we fought—and who knows how long it had been since the faerie took over.

"Oh yes," Castiel tries to say casually. "We were wondering who that might be." Either he does a poor job of concealing his anger, or I've come to learn his body language.

"*What did he look like?*" Euphelia's wild voice pierces through my fog of anger, but it does nothing to calm the rage in my heart.

"Give us the wish for having completed the Challenge, and perhaps we will tell you," I snarl.

"You aren't particularly in the position to negotiate, are you?" Ryken scoffs, though his eyes flash with anger.

"And you are?"

"We most certainly are," his lips curl with disdain before his face smooths over again, nonchalance replacing already thinly veiled anger. "You have not completed the Challenge. The magic will not let us grant your wish even if we wanted to."

"But you can easily just *leave*," I growl.

"Why would we do that?" He purrs, and I feel hatred bury itself deep in my veins.

"Because it's the right thing to do, *unlike* sending us on an impossible mission knowing we could not complete it."

His eyes narrow and darken. "Like I was trying to say, our doubts were not of that vein." He straightens and leans back. "Regardless, you have failed the Trial Challenge. The Day Court is now ours."

Fury burns in my heart and spreads through my body. Castiel growls quietly beside me, but it's muffled to my ears.

They sent us on a quest knowing it could not be completed. They sent us on a hunt knowing that someone would emerge—that its corpse would burn to ashes. They dangled a shred of hope in front of us like bait and let us chase it.

Something in me snaps.

This is *wrong*; this is not the brand of justice I want to live with, and I will not accept failure.

As much as I despise and fear queenship, as much as I know I am not fit for the position, I also know that *these* siblings should not rule, either. They would only let the court wither and wilt.

Just imagining the Day Court looking anything like the ruins of the Lunar Court has my blood boiling.

My next words tumble out before I can stop them, because I'm not thinking about being queen—I'm thinking about making sure the court does not die.

That this piece of Asteria will remain safe from their vile clutches.

That our homes are not ravaged.

"I invoke the Challenge."

CHAPTER SIXTEEN

EVERY PAIR OF EYES swings toward me.

Castiel stares at me with horror. Whether it is because he knows I don't want to be queen, or whether he's furious that I would take this from him, I can't tell. I only hope he doesn't think I've betrayed him. Not after what we've been through. Not after what he's revealed to me.

I focus on the tang of magic that spreads on my tongue and stare unflinchingly at Ryken.

His eyes narrow, but his lips pull into a smirk.

"Are you sure you want to do this?" He asks. "For *him*? Out of all the princes you could have chosen, I am still surprised you went with this one."

Castiel does not rise to the goad, but spins to look at me instead. He works his jaw, and I can see the conflict in his eyes. I see that he's not horrified at the idea I have betrayed him—he doesn't think that at all.

He's worried about *me*.

I can't stand to meet his gaze for long. Knowing the golden prince that once bullied me now worries and cares for me makes my soul wrench in an uncomfortable way that I don't have time to bother figuring out right now.

Ryken takes my silence as acceptance and rolls his shoulders. "When would you like to carry out the Challenge? It'll take some time to get the word out and gather the spectators. I presume you'll—"

"Today," I growl. "We end this today."

His eyebrows arch, and the dark smirk widens.

EVERY COURT HAS SEVERAL fields for sparring practice, but each court has one field specifically reserved only for Challenges.

We walk through the Day grounds until we reach a large, uncovered field of dirt. Beyond it are more fields just like it; we've arrived at the far end of the castle grounds where faeries can train without disturbing civilization.

Castiel and Rowan flank me on each side, but neither of us speak. Ahead, Ryken and Euphelia chat loudly, as if blissfully carefree.

Their voices sound muffled to my ears as I take deep breaths to calm my racing heart.

This is my element. Combat is where I feel most comfortable—most like myself.

Yet, a part of me cannot help but remember that Euphelia and Ryken led the charge and defeated the entire Day Court's castle in one quick, devastating night.

Not only is that a testament to their skill and ability, but to their prowess for unifying even the wildest and most chaotic fae.

Perhaps *that* scares me more.

Ryken and I face each other on the field. It's a little larger than the usual ones used for running laps and sparring practice, but that works to my advantage because I'm quick. The sun beats down against my back, and for a moment I wonder if the sun is hotter in the Day Court or if my nerves are acting up.

I clench my fist and swallow. Fighting is something I've always been good at. I beat every student in my year at the Academy. Ryken might be older and more experienced, but I know I can do this.

Just breathe. Stay calm and learn his movements. Learn his cues, just like you always do.

Euphelia, Castiel, and Rowan stand off to one side as witnesses. Now that we're here, I almost regret initiating the Challenge so quickly because there's no time to inform my sisters or my mother.

Almost.

Castiel's placed his mask of insouciance back on, but I can tell from the way his shoulders are set that he's worried.

I don't blame him. This has to be one of the most impulsive things I've ever done.

Rowan paces back and forth before sitting at Castiel's side again, letting the princeling dig his hand into the dark fur. As much as Castiel claims to hate his court, it's still a part of him. It's where he grew up. It's his home.

And most of all, it's a part of Asteria—*my* home.

I won't let it wither and die. I won't let it become like the Lunar Court.

When I win, we will return victorious to share the joyous news. And then, I will have to figure out a way to inform my family that I am leaving the Night Court to become...

I shake those thoughts out of my mind. I will deal with that if I win.

Once I win, I correct myself.

We signal we are ready, and a deafening crack of lightning hurtles downward from the sky: a sign from Sirona and the land signifying the start of the Challenge.

Significantly more dramatic than the start of our Trial Challenge—I try not to see it as a bad omen.

The bolt of blue-white energy strikes the ground and creates a cloud of dust in its wake. I squint to see through it, but it's impossible to penetrate the dusty veil.

Suddenly, Ryken emerges, cutting through the cloud before it even settles.

He does not hesitate; he charges faster than I thought was possible for fae.

His face is vicious, and his teeth are bared. Black lightning surrounds his fist.

I barely have time to react, sidestepping out of the way and summoning my sword from my reserve.

In the excitement, I'd forgotten that I hadn't extinguished the everfyre. Its blue glow nearly blinds me, but it surprises Ryken, too.

I recover before he does and charge at him, slashing my sword downward.

A sword blinks into existence in his hands at the last moment, and I grit my teeth as the clang of metal on metal shoots up my arms.

In my periphery, I notice black sparkles in his left hand.

I retreat just in time to see that he's now holding a dagger as well as his sword.

He grins like a madman, and I falter.

In one breath, he's on me—his dagger inches from my stomach, held back only by my sword.

He's fast. Not as fast as Freyin, but my body isn't reacting the way it normally does.

I dart back and forth, dodging and learning his cues—and acutely aware that I am much slower than usual.

I am tired from the journey, but I made an emotional decision, and now I must follow through.

Whatever is happening to me isn't a result of our battle with the Forescua. By the time we left the little cabin, I had already been healed. Castiel made sure of it and then made me rest a little extra just for good measure. I'd felt fine until we stepped onto the battlefield.

Until I started using magic.

I send magic down my left arm and white-silver flames burst forth, hurtling toward the Dark faerie.

Ryken doesn't bother with a shield, choosing instead to dash between my magical attacks with ease.

I'm unflustered—my goal is to watch how he moves.

But the magic takes more out of me than I expect; my entire left arm tingles. Growling, I shake it off and refocus my attention.

Only to realize he's disappeared.

I look around. The field is empty.

But our spectators are looking up.

At the last moment, I duck and sidestep—but not fast enough.

His sword clips my shoulder and rips down my right arm. Pain explodes, and I instinctively put distance between us though I've dropped my sword.

No matter.

I don't have time to stitch myself up, so I summon two daggers instead—they're smaller and easier to hold despite the furious fire that rips through my side.

I imbue both blades with sparkling silver magic and throw one after another, summoning a second pair as soon as the first sail toward him.

In this fashion, I throw four more blades in succession.

He dodges the first five, but I twist my wrist and send my last dagger to where he *will* be, rather than where he *is*.

Ryken grunts when my blade buries itself deep into his shoulder.

We spend the next moments in an evenly matched dance. Each time one of us loses a weapon, the other does as well.

Eventually, we lock ourselves into a fistfight, our weapons lost in the battlefield, with neither of us able to recall them.

He swings and I duck. I sweep my leg and he barely jumps in time—so I twist my body and catch him behind the knee with my foot.

He crumples. I send magic to my legs and knee him in the face, sending him backwards.

I hop on him and straddle his chest to ready myself for the finishing blow. Magic ripples under my skin, aching and burning to be released. It licks my arm hotter than I've ever felt.

Swirling blue patterns blossom on my arms, glowing.

I falter, and the markings disappear along with my magic sinking back under my skin.

Ryken's face is a bloody mess, and his hair is all over the place. He's staring death in the eyes, and yet... there is the hint of a smirk on his face.

A strange light in his eyes—a mad delight that sparkles, almost like he *enjoys* this.

The pure fire in his eyes makes me hesitate again. In that moment, he catches me off guard.

He flips us and punches me hard in the jaw. I see stars, but I don't need my sight to wrap my arms around his and use his own momentum against him.

I throw him off balance and dart to the side, wiping the blood from my forehead.

We stand, facing each other.

He has a wild grin—a vastly different look from when we first started. Ryken wipes the blood from his mouth and spits out more.

"Do you feel it?" He asks. The edge in his eyes makes me uncomfortable. "The electricity. We have a connection..."

"Yeah," I say. "My fist to your face."

I charge my hands up with magic. Before I can lunge, something burns. Not the regular heat of magic rippling under my skin, but something *more*.

Something *not right*.

"I think I love you." His eyes glow against the setting sun, a strange look on his face.

"*What*?" My head snaps up to meet his wild gaze, all focus lost from calling magic.

"No one has ever fought me like this before." He sweeps his hand around the battlefield to our littered weapons. The holes we've wrought on the ground. The marks of our fight. "No one

A TWIST OF NIGHT AND DAY

has come close to defeating me. No one has been my equal, and yet here you are."

I blink hard. "Are you really so broken and unloved that you think being beat is a form of affection?"

"Yes," he says confidently. The quirk of his lips tells me he is being true. There is no hint of deception on his sharp face.

I'm about to answer, but the burning in my hands distracts me. The blaze starts at my fingertips and spreads until it consumes my entire body and all I see is white.

Nothing but white hot pain.

My legs crumble.

I bite my lip to keep from crying out as I drop to my knees.

I squeeze my eyes shut and open them again, but my vision is blurred. Ryken's violet eyes widen in shock, and even he stills to watch.

Horror pools in my stomach when I notice blue lines glowing on my hands. They've not only returned—they've spread from my palms to the back of my hands and all the way up my arms. I know that if I had a mirror, I'd see them on my face, too.

I swing to meet Castiel's gaze. I see my own fear reflected in his terrified cobalt eyes.

Something collides with my cheek, and I get a mouthful of dirt.

Ryken pins me down, though it's not like I can move, anyway. His wild, purple eyes burn with a heat I don't understand.

But I do recognize the black flames on his fists.

I can't move.

My entire body is on fire.

Pain wracks through every fiber of my being, and it's all I can do to stop myself from begging someone—anyone—to end it. I want to curl into a ball and beg for it to stop.

I want to shut my eyes, but I have to watch as my death comes. I want him to look me in the eye as he kills me.

And I know he will; my rejection must have further fueled his anger and hatred of me. Men don't like to be rejected.

My eyes meet his.

I forget all pain for one singular moment as he speaks, a different kind of fire in his heated, violet gaze.

"Marry me."

A SNEAK PEEK OF BOOK 2...

WITHOUT ANY MAGIC, my chances of escaping are bleak and getting worse by the day.

Unfortunately for me, I sit across from the siblings at a pristine, white table out in the Day Castle's gardens.

Euphelia's bright red lips curl up in a sneer before hiding it behind a teacup. Her purple eyes flicker away from me as if I'm no longer worth a thought.

Her nails are painted just as red, and she wears her sleek hair pulled up today except for two pitch black strands that curl in front.

And though her eyes look away, I can feel another pair pinned on me.

I refuse to meet those violet seas.

Even though I am extremely curious as to where the siblings have been for the majority of these past two weeks, I spear another piece of fruit with my fork and pray they leave. I've learned that whenever Ryken speaks to me, he asks the same obnoxious question of whether I'm ready.

Ready to be his bride.

A growl of annoyance almost escapes from my lips just from the thought. I stab a grape and pretend it's his head.

"Astrid," his dark voice purrs.

"No," I say between gritted teeth.

"You don't even know what I was going to say."

I drag my eyes up to meet his and raise an eyebrow. Amusement lights in his eyes; his delight at my discomfort brings a storm of rage into my heart that I have to work hard to keep hidden.

I can endure this. I survived the Academy as a social pariah, and I can survive here. Granted, I had my magic and the knowledge that I would return home to my family back then.

But it's okay. I can find a way out.

"I don't even know why you deign to look at her," Euphelia drawls. "She's not particularly strong or pretty."

"Take these magic silencers off wrists, and we can see who's stronger," I growl. If Euphelia is anything like Ryken, I don't know that I can beat her. But she's annoying enough that I would die trying.

Her dark eyes peer at me past her teacup, which she then sets down. "You're foolish to think my brother would truly be interested in you."

"I hope he *isn't* interested in me," I fire back and glare at Ryken, who only smirks at the exchange.

"My two favorite women getting along."

"Why don't you get out of here and go back to whatever you guys were up to?" I feign innocence and bat my lashes for good measure. If anger and frustration make him happy, then I'd gladly swing the other way. "I'm sure you have much destroying and pillaging to do," I add sweetly.

That got Euphelia's attention. She stiffens and glares.

Ryken doesn't seem affected. "Are you saying you miss us?"

My sweet smile almost cracks and I bite my tongue to keep from snarling, but I realize this is a good opportunity to try and fish for information about what they've been up to.

I force my lips to stay pulled in a smile. "Just wondering how long you'll be away next and what you're up to in that time."

"Fixing your mistake," Euphelia's eyes narrow.

Ryken's head shifts sharply toward his sister, but the motion is so minute I'm not sure it happens at all. There's something they're not telling me, and I want to find out what it is.

"What mistake?" I continue as if I hadn't noticed Ryken's reaction.

Her eyes flicker to meet her brother's, and she crosses her arms. "None of your business, halfling."

I struggle to keep the smile plastered on my face as I respond. "Sirona forbid something happens during one of your outings and I'm stuck here, alone forever."

A scowl mars her pretty face. She stands up so fast the chair skids backward, nearly toppling over. "Let's go," she nods at her brother before leaving without a second look at me.

Ryken stares at me with an odd smile on his face before he stands up to follow his sister back into the castle, leaving me to fume at my breakfast alone.

I'd won this battle, but I'm still losing the war.

WANT TO HEAR THE TITLE OF BOOK 2 BEFORE ANYONE ELSE? Sign up for Aubrey's newsletter at:
https://aubreywinters.com/subscribe

WHILE YOU WAIT FOR BOOK 2, take a look at another of Aubrey's books, LIFE BOUND:

"When a vampire throws you out of a window, don't make him your personal bodyguard."

mybook.to/lifebound

CONNECT WITH AUBREY!

https://aubreywinters.com
https://instagram.com/authoraubreywinters/
https://vm.tiktok.com/ZMeuVnB59/

BOOKS BY AUBREY WINTERS

The Shadow World series
Life Bound
Soul Bound

The Asteria Chronicles
A Twist of Night and Day

Printed in Great Britain
by Amazon